WELSH FLANNEL

Welsh Flannel

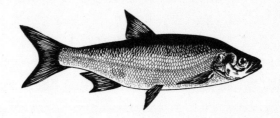

Derek Brock

ISIS
LARGE PRINT
Oxford

First published in Great Britain 2002
by ISIS Publishing Ltd,
7 Centremead, Osney Mead, Oxford OX2 0ES
by arrangement with Derek Brock

British Library Cataloguing in Publication Data
Brock, Derek
    Welsh flannel. – Large print ed.
    1. City and town life – Wales – Fiction 2. Large type books
    I. Title
    823.9'2[F]

ISBN 0-7531-6579-1 (hb)
ISBN 0-7531-6580-5 (pb)

Printed and bound by Antony Rowe, Chippenham and Reading

CONTENTS

Prologue

At the very top of the Rhondda and beyond lies the jewel of the Gilfach Mawr. A Welsh folk fantasy for all who will read these chronicles.

Compare yourself to an Olympian god, a Celtic Zeus if you like, and gaze down upon the inhabitants of this Welsh Shangri-la set in a bowl of hills away from all intrusion. Seen only by your eyes, not from the azure heavens over Crete but through the rain clouds of the Rhondda, an ancient hearse approaches the town. The blue tinged hands and long boney fingers of Morgan the Morgue hold the shaking steering wheel as the vehicle struggles along the common road. His son Idris studies with bated breath the suspended dewdrop at the tip of his huge curved nose, vein matted, like a London underground map. The black silk of their top hats shines with a morbid lustre in the late afternoon sun, whilst the barathea of their frocktail coats are faded green with age on the shoulders.

"I tell you now, Idris," says the father, in a muffled tone as his large red spotted handkerchief arrests the tantalising liquid crystal pendant. "You can't use them fancy marketing techniques in this sort of business, I reckon you wasted your money on that correspondence course, that's what I reckon."

His son gazes contemplatively at a flock of mountain sheep busily engaged in foraging spilled refuse bins, thinking that perhaps that is the secret of their succulent flavour and not their diet of mountain herbs so eagerly publicised by butcher Mordicai from his shop in the high street.

"Got to keep up with the times, mun," he replies. "Look at the Co-op, how they've got on, biggest undertakers in the country, an' they gives divi on their burials too. That's a Marketing Technique, innit?"

Jacob Morgan turns his head to face him, his large bloodshot eyes full of emotional temperament above layers of watery bags reaching as far as his prominent cheekbones.

"But they haven't used people like Pritchard the Brush with his fancy sign-writing. I tell you that hoarding has got to come down, it's vulgar, that's what it is, Lord knows what they think of it up at Ebenezer Chapel."

"Well, what's wrong with it? Pritchard only gave it a touch of colour."

The old man winces.

"Touch of colour! Used to be black and gold, all full of misery and sorrow like, now look at it — fluorescent disco colours and the wording, oh my God." The hearse swerves violently as his hands leave the wheel in a gesture of woe. "It's worse than the supermarkets down in Ponty."

His hand instinctively touches the brim of his hat as they enter the town and Bessie Price the organist of

Ebenezer looks up with a smile from her step-polishing ritual. Its slate grey shines with a lustre unrivalled in the whole of Taff Street to crown her the undisputed champion of Gilfach. At the end of the street of shining steps, past the cliff-face graveyard of Ebenezer, with headstones poised like precarious dominoes, stands the iron citadel of prosperity. Like an Eiffel Tower with a wheel, it symbolises the very existence of the valley, at the same time that it undermines the community in a constant search for the black gold beneath. Behind it, like a dark grey Matterhorn with an ever-growing pinnacle, is the Gilfach slag heap, served day and night by a procession of squeaking aerial drams. In winter it serves as a rather dirty cable car to the crest of the Gilfach run, where sheets of corrugated iron imitate the glossy bobsleighs of the more famous Cresta.

Past the miners' welfare hall, built completely of inscribed foundation stones from grateful coal owners of yesteryear, onto the Labour Club, the Conservative Club and the Marxist Club, all with members of doubtful loyalty trickling through their political portals for the morning tipple. From the open door of Franchiani's Temperance Cafe comes the piercing scream of the espresso pipe in duet to a Verdi aria from the Welsh Neapolitan. To the rarefied atmosphere of Mount Pleasant struggles the steaming Daimler, toward the chapel of rest where Mrs Morgan sings her way through a workload of daily chores, unchanged since the first day of her marriage to the young Gilfach undertaker.

3

She glances into the front room as she polishes the tiled pavement of the hall floor. There Lewis the Draper lies peacefully at rest in his expensive oak casket.

"Won't be long now, Mr Evans," she pauses to say during her singing. "Half past two you're going. Idris is on his way back this minute to see to you, like. Soon as they've had their dinner you'll be on your way. Laver bread and bacon today, they wouldn't miss that if they was burying royalty."

She walks into the room to gaze down on the old man.

"Dew, Dew, Mr Lewis, there's peaceful and young you look, never take you for ninety. Damn it don't seem like yesterday when I used to come into your shop for a length of knicker elastic, and that was forty years ago. Three farthings a yard it was then." Her serene face changes to a smile. "Good stuff it was too, Mr Lewis, too good in fact, my brother Jenkin was always stealinig it for his catapult."

Her solitude is suddenly broken with the high-pitched tone of Ivor Pritchard as he taps the bay window with the shaft of his sign-writer's brush.

"Sorry to interrupt your conversation, Mrs Morgan, but I can't get it all in, the easy term slogan, I mean, 'Die now, pay later' — it's too long for large lettering, like."

Mrs Morgan holds her hands over the corpse's ears.

"Pritchard, where's your manners, people like Mr Lewis would never hear of H.P. I don't know what have got into young Idris with his fancy ideas, I'm sure I don't."

4

Pritchard's face takes on a puzzled expression at her action.

"Only fighting competition, he is, Mrs Morgan. The big boys 'ave got it all sewn up, like, it's no longer a part-time fiddle of the small builder."

Mrs Morgan walks over to the half-open window.

"But he don't know when to stop, Pritchard, look what he sends out with the accounts."

She holds a black edged card up to the painter and he reads aloud

"'Ten per cent off your next funeral with this special valued customer voucher'. Well, that's what they call initiative, Mrs Morgan."

Suddenly she is summoned by the high-pitched scream of the whistling kettle to the shrine of the house, the black-leaded altar where the elixir of life is brewed. Beneath the deep red velvet fringe of the mantelpiece that carries two brass candlesticks, four Staffordshire pottery horsemen, two jade vases and the silent Westminster chiming clock that conceals the rent book and insurance cards, glows the very soul of the dwelling. It reaches out with comforting warmth to continue the mottling of Mrs Morgan's varicosed legs, whilst its upward heat gently waves the damp washing on the brass rail above like limp flags.

She fills the teapot in preparation for her daily ritual of reading the horoscopes. The headlines of ten newspapers are ignored as she races through their pages to discover her fate for twenty-four hours. She fondles a copper pendant of Aries as one astrologer contradicts the next, but she is undaunted: the law of averages supports her faith in the cult. After the fourth tepid cup of tea, she stacks the bale of identical newsprint on the shining surface of the American-cloth covered kitchen table during a mental survey. Her face blooms slowly into a broad smile of exuberance as she talks aloud.

"Dew, Dew, mun, six in favour of booking a holiday abroad, I'll have him down to Jones the Travel today if I have to take him in the hearse myself. Stick in the mud, that's what he is. Porthcawl it have been for thirty years, but I've had enough. An independent woman I'll be in three weeks, liberated at sixty by my pension."

Meanwhile, her aged beau studies his face in the driving mirror as the Collier's Arms draws near. He decides that his nose has lost a shade of its purple hue, and it requires a recharge. The hearse squeaks to a welcome halt at the door. The bar reeks with its usual morning aroma of immovable stale smoke and beer, pine sawdust and disinfectant. Like a cooling meteor, the huge slow combustion stove at the centre of the room pulsates, throwing a welcome glow on Morgan's hyperthermic frame.

Crevice Hughes, the landlord with a concave face, surveys his customers with a gummy smile as his painful set of false ivories snarl, imprisoned in their pint pot of water beneath the counter.

"Firewater, Mr Morgan?" he asks in a wet, pliable diction.

"If you please," answers the undertaker, bestowing a weak smile at the row of regulars behind the long, scrubbed table. They are Pitprop Parry, representing most of the power in the Gilfach rugby team, Non-Ferrous Jones the rag and bone dealer, Evans the Bus, Espresso Franchiani the Temperance Café, seeking refuge from his celebrated dandelion and burdock, and Loose Edna James, in a permanent state of futile solicitation to satisfy her fantasies.

Morgan's dull eyes take on a sparkle as they feast on her forty-year old thighs through the provocative torn slit of her tweed skirt. The daily erotic vision has been the sole appeasement for his lust for the past fifteen years, and she accepts his rewarding bottle of stout like the bordello queen of her dreams.

"No vice in Gilfach," she whispers loudly to Evans the Bus. "They're not ready for it yet, but he'll come round to it one of these days."

The undertaker, with a new complexion to his nose, leaves slowly for his laver bread lunch and his business with Mr Lewis the Draper, deceased. Later in the afternoon, the organ of Ebenezer vibrates the very nails from the pitchpine rafters above, the hawk-faced Bessie Price smiling serenely as she presses the keys for "Bread of Heaven" , and all but the deceased purveyor of knicker elastic render forth with gusto when suddenly the vibrant organ begins to lose its dominance as the notes develop a wheezing discord.

Behind the fascia of gold-leaf pipes, Giliard Pugh the organ pumper has begun to develop one of his nervous itching attacks. The irritation leaves no part of his body sacred as he prays for the multi-hands of a heathen statue. He is galvanized by the voice of Gladys Price as she hisses "Pump, Giliard, pump, will you?"

7

He dutifully divides his attentions with a pump and a scratch, causing the hymn to come and go like a radio with a dodgy volume control. As your eyes travel along the faces of the bemused congregation, they see more of the cast of the saga to follow. The buxom Winnie Purvis, forewoman and WX model for the corset and bra factory. Minerva Harris, mousetrap assembler at the Gilfach wire works, with painfully slender legs and a fetish for high heels: who can resist her nickname of Minnie Mouse? Evans the Herbalist capitalises with his anti-death pills literature to the annoyance of Jones the Spy, chairman of the Karl Marx Social Club, who is reputed to phone Moscow weekly.

They play their game of choral hide and seek with the intermittent organ and the loud tipping of miners' free coal to the neat terrace of houses across the road. Diehard Davies, the Conservative Club chairman, pauses to console his wife as he barrows his fuel through the parlour.

"Too bloody houseproud, that's your trouble, missus. You either have the place clean and cold or dirty and warm. Just let me know and I'll sell the coal next door, straight from the gutter, like. That's capitalism, that is."

Three doors away, in the corrugated iron community hall, Jones the Knot surveys his afternoon yoga class with a sensuous pride as he walks between the rows of plough-postured buttocks to scowl at the boney posterior of Acne Rees, the only male of his class. Up at the Temperance Billiard Hall, near the river bridge where black colliery water cascades like shimmering tar

8

over a reef of old cycles, prams and washing machines, old Danny Pot Black irons the green baize of a vacant table, his brown woollen cardigan once the length of his waist now sagging below his knees with the weight of the coinage takings in each pocket.

Near the end of the road, the little stone primary school shudders with released emotion as its inmates take their afternoon break. Small boys in the urinal make wagers of bubble gum and sweets on the power of their penis to eject over the dividing wall, where undaunted, Israel Jones the religious maniac daubs his bible graffitti beneath an umbrella.

Across the square, beyond the statue of Lloyd George, in James the Gents' Outfitters, Nancy-Boy Adams measures inside legs with reckless abandon. From her boutique window nearby, Brenda Pugh frowns with envy and Price the Prudential cycles past, immune to her desire for feminine equality and the day that she can be a gents' tailor.

In the chemist, behind his three massive flasks of coloured water, Davies the Dispenser softens a baby rusk in his daily tipple of iron tonic wine, whilst district nurse Esther Parry looks on with contempt for the depraved excesses of her lover.

"You never forget that, Idwal, do you?" she whispers loudly, snapping the closure of her black bag. "I only wish I could attract the same attention. Evans the Herbalist sees me in a different light, mind you, but I can't stand his wind, makes out he can cure death, but he got nothing for that."

In the police station, Sergeant Emrys Pritchard adjusts the mirror on his desk to capture policewoman Dilys Jenkins in the next room as she straightens her seams right up to her thighs. Up at the council library Mr Basingstoke, the Librarian from England no less, looks down with scorn on the Gilfach rugby club below his office window, where a flock of sheep prepare the sacred turf of the ninety degree pitch for Saturday's match.

"Not a pitch," he grumbles through a surprised belch of nervous wind. "It's a damn obstacle course."

Down at the Miners' Welfare Hall, the Welsh Language Operatic Society rehearse the only score available, "Merry England", hastily translated into their native tongue for the forthcoming St David's Day festival while the night begins to shroud the little town, with an Orphean veil of decency over 36 Pant Street where twenty women of all ages cram the small parlour for a sex aid party. The huge mass of Gwyneth Maylor vibrates like a blancmange effigy as she holds a suit of black rubber to her audience.

"I don't think this would do much for my Edwin, girls, he'd take me for a pile of car tyres like."

And in his splendid bungalow on the green hillside of planning taboo, Wyndham Pugh Davies the town clerk broaches the subject of wife-swapping as his small, close eyes swiftly avoid the leathery features of his spouse in favour of Gwendoline Toogood, his neighbour's succulent mistress.

"It's quite rife in the smaller townships," he squeaks in an eager tone. "No doubt it will reach Gilfach before long, I'm afraid."

And the common law wife Miss Toogood responds with a condescending smile to her common law husband, whose secret shame is the talk of Gilfach.

From the darkness of her bedroom window, spinster Edith Lloyd teeters dangerously on a three-leg stool as her maiden eyes peer down into the circular red brick urinal of Gilfach Square, then forlornly back to the double bed of her fantasies.

But even the prying eyes of nosey Celtic gods need rest, so let us sleep and return tomorrow to the warmth of our Welsh Flannel.

CHAPTER
ONE

The Three Piece Suit

Nancy Boy Adams had decided to expand his tailoring business and home shopping was the answer.

"Yes," he said to himself as he minced around the shop with his feather duster. "Brutus Adams will take his business to the customer."

He whispered his Christian name in dislike. Why had his father, a six foot six ex-guardsman, later a sergeant of the constabulary, cursed him with such a masculine name? For that matter, why had his father requested a transfer to the farthest outpost of the constabulary when he told him that he was "different?"

"I had great plans for you, boyo!" he exploded as his face became scarlet. "The guards, the police and the rugby team and then you tells me you're a bloody queer. Your mother put you up to this, that's for sure. Dressed you too much in pink when you was in the pram. I had a feeling it would turn your head."

Later that morning he scribbled various versions of his advertisement for the *Valley Times*. He would launch his venture with a new name and he decided on "Valley Home Shopping Service." The opening offer would be a fine tailor-made gents suit, but creative writing was far from young Adams's forte and what appeared in the Valley Times was quite remote from his original intentions.

The first and only reply came from Hermit Rees, a retired collier, who lived on top of the Gilfach mountain in a corrugated iron bungalow. He rarely came into town and had no knowledge of the entrepreneur behind the Valley Home Shopping Service.

That evening Brutus closed his shop with excited anticipation of the first sale of his new venture. He checked his appearance before leaving and smiled with approval at the camp male in the mirror.

"Hermit Rees will have a shock" he said to himself as he struck various poses. "He'll expect one of the common valley pack men to arrive and I shall appear just like an apparition from Hollywood."

* * *

Large flakes of snow began to place a white shroud over the outline of his minute Austin Seven saloon as he pulled away from the square, and Brutus suffered pangs of apprehension as his little car made heavy weather of the going over the snow-clad climb to the home of Hermit Rees, which eventually appeared as a Christmas card scene, with a welcome light from its solitary window. He stepped from his vehicle into a foot of snow, completely immersing his black and white brogues and silk socks. Lifting his trousers by their knees, he tiptoed to the front door and used the heavy cast iron knocker to cause a small avalanche that totally enshrouded him in snow.

The enthusiasm for his new venture was rapidly declining when the door opened to reveal Hermit Rees, a giant of a man brandishing a double barrel shotgun.

His voice screamed like a circular saw tearing through a log. "You selling double glazing or something?"

Brutus began to stammer a reply but the twin barrels came ominously near to his nose.

"Well, you're one of those Bible preachers, is you?"

"No. No!" pleaded Brutus in a voice laden with fear. "I'm the representative from the Valley Home Shopping Service. You asked me to call. Look here. I got your letter, like. It was our advert in the *Valley Times*, see."

Hermit Rees pointed his gun towards the interior of the bungalow. "Come on in, then. You picked a hell of a night to call. You must be hard-up for business, that's all I can say."

Brutus followed the huge man into a cosy living room where a glowing red fire began to create steam from his sodden clothing. He placed his small case on the table and began to open it. Hermit Rees fingered a piece of pinstripe from the sample book. "Bit flimsy, init?" he said with a glare of contempt.

"Oh, they get a lot heavier, Mr Rees," answered Brutus. "It's all a matter of personal choice, see," and he quickly flicked the cloth pages to the back of the swatch to reveal some thick Harris Tweed specimens.

"That's better" said Hermit. "I'll have it in that cloth. Something substantial like, init."

"A good choice," answered Brutus, his face beaming with success at the thought of the first sale of his new enterprise. "Now then, Mr Rees. Will you bend your right arm so that I can measure it, please?"

Hermit's blue-scarred face showed a puzzled expression as the tailor took his arm measurement before jotting it down in his note pad.

"Right, Mr Rees," continued Brutus. "Now we'll take your inside leg length, if you don't mind. Legs slightly apart, please, Mr Rees, while I hold the tape to your thigh."

Suddenly Brutus felt as if a mechanical grab, like the ones from the colliery, had grasped his neck and flung him across the room.

"I thought there was something funny about you" said Hermit Rees as he towered over him. "You're one of them nancy boys. That's what you are. I knew they was in Cardiff but never Gilfach."

"I was only doing my job, Mr Rees!" stammered the terrified Brutus.

"Well, you're not doing your bloody job on me, boyo, that's for sure." said Hermit as he took Brutus by his neck. "I'm going to lock you up till the snow clears. I can't trust you hanging around outside. I'd never rest in me bed like."

He carried Brutus with the ease of a suit on a coat hanger to the corrugated iron coal house afew yards from the house. As he landed painfully on the hard pile of house coal, Brutus heard an ominous click of a padlock and began to realise that this would be his cell until the mountain road was usable for his welcome return to Gilfach.

Dawn appeared through a crack in the door to reveal the sad picture of a once immaculate Brutus, now a dishevelled blackened figure on his torturous bed of coal.

"Never again will I enter a strange man's house." he murmured to himself. "The man's a maniac" he said aloud with indignation. "What harm can I do just by measuring him for a suit? I've measured hundreds of legs in my time and this is the first time that I've ended up in a coal house. The man's mad. Must have an obsession about his legs being touched, even with his trousers on."

The click of the door lock interrupted his verbal misery to reveal the giant frame of Hermit holding a plate of evil smelling boiled fish.

"Here's some toe rag for your breakfast. Don't want you dying of starvation on me. The wireless says it's going to thaw later, then you can bugger off and don't come near me again. Measure my legs, indeed. I've never heard of such a thing, like something from the *News of the World*. That's what it is."

Brutus couldn't escape from the obnoxious smell of his breakfast. He buried it beneath the coal but the persistent odour, similar to that of the Clydach knacker's yard, still pervaded every inch of the small coal house.

It was mid-afternoon before Hermit Rees reappeared holding a copy of the *Valley Times*. His large nose snorted vapour in the cold air like an angry bull.

"Look. I've found your advert," he bellowed. "You're no more a furniture salesman than my foot. You're a sex maniac, you are. Getting into people's houses under false pretence by using this advert."

"Furniture salesman?" queried Brutus. "I'm not a furniture salesman. I'm a gent's outfitter."

"Well, it don't say that here" replied Hermit as he held the newspaper before Brutus. "Look. It's as plain as the nose on my face. Buy a three piece suite complete in the comfort of your own home. So why would you want to measure my legs for a suite of furniture? I tell you. You're a nancy boy just using this advert to get in my house and abuse me."

Brutus peered at the newspaper through the shaft of daylight that surrounded Hermit's giant frame. Had he made the mistake or was that the newspaper's fault? But whoever did it had spelt "suit" with an "e" at the end. No wonder Hermit was upset. He thought he was buying furniture.

That evening, an unwashed and untidy man enrolled at the Clydach adult night class for reading lessons.

But spelling was decidedly not his forte. For six months later he launched his summer sale with a large self produced poster in his shop window. It read:

"Three piece soots half price."

CHAPTER
TWO

Short Back and Sides

Trevor Evans sat in his barber's chair and spoke to his reflection in the mirror that faced him.

"You've had it, butty. Stylists they call themselves these day. The short back and sides is finished save for a few pensioners."

His training as an Army barber had earned him a living for forty years but now customers wanted all sorts of "Hair Design" as they called it. Each time he returned from a pensioner's funeral, he could see his takings decline.

"What do she know about hair cuts?" he said of the young lady who recently opened her "Salon" in the square. "Unisex!" he spat the word at the mirror in contempt. "Sounds more like a brothel than a hairdresser's. Spends an hour on a bloke to give him a head like a lavatory brush. Gawd help us. I could do a whole platoon down to the wood in a morning. As fast as a sheep shearer I was in those days. Even had an offer from the Company Commander when I was demobbed. Two thousand sheep he had. 'If you can keep the regiment so well shorn, you're good enough for my sheep,' he said." Trevor sighed "Should have taken him at his word. The sheep haven't changed their ways. No fancy styling for them. It's still all off."

He rose from the chair to escape from his depressed face and aimlessly thumbed through the tattered pages of a Tit Tat magazine. His hand automatically began to caress his skin-tight hairless head as he read the exciting headline of an article.

"*Chicken droppings can cure baldness.*" It was one of those accidental discoveries whereby a young poultry farmer had fallen into the manure pit of his battery unit. It took more than an hour before the Fire Brigade eventually dragged his near lifeless body from the evil-smelling mass that had tried to claim him.

But as Newton discovered gravity by accident, so did this young man realise the hair-growing properties of chicken manure. He was already the proud possessor of a fine head of hair, but as the days of his convalescence progressed he noticed a growth of hair appearing over the whole of his body. Within a month he took on the appearance of a gorilla and he realised that he had discovered Man's greatest desire. A hair restorer!

His ethos, however, was short lived and doomed to failure by the Health and Safety Act, which forbade the use of sewerage in preparations for the human body. The article closed with the news that the poultry farmer "is now happily employed in a circus as a human gorilla".

Trevor spoke to himself as he placed the magazine back on the seat. "Should have kept it all to himself. He would have made a million out of it."

That evening he called at the small holding of Beaky Jones, a name earned through a lifetime with chickens.

"I got to diversify," he shouted at Beaky above the noise of a thousand clucking hens as they strolled through the battery house. "That young piece in town have ruined my trade with her fancy hair cuts. I been thinking of drying chicken dung and selling it in fancy bags as a fertiliser, like," he lied.

Beaky's eyes glowed in the low light of the poultry shed. The bane of his life had always been the disposal of his chicken manure. No-one wanted it. It was too strong as a fertiliser and over the years he had accrued a small mountain of it.

"I got about a hundred ton. You can have it in a job lot for fifty quid."

On an impulse Trevor had instantly smoothed the shiny skin of his cranium while all around him a thousand marauding hens expelled magic gold from their rectums to transfer a million bald domes to hairy objects of delight.

"Done!' said Trevor in a glorious cloud of elation.

"Where would you like it delivered?" replied Beaky, rubbing his hands in glee.

"I thought I'd take a car-boot load as I want it," answered Trevor.

"No. I need the room see," said Beaky. "That's why I'm letting you have it so cheap, like."

"Well, let's see if it will fit into my backyard," Trevor replied with a frown as they both walked toward the hundred ton mound of potential hair restorer. He gazed up to the peak where a wisp of steam curled from the apex.

21

"Like a miniature Vesuvius, init?" said Beaky. "A sleeping giant just waiting to erupt. It's gold that will make you a very rich man."

Trevor was convinced. He shook Beaky by the hand. "The deal's done, then. Fifty Four Pant Street, lane entrance."

"That'll be another hundred quid for delivery charges," said Beaky with a half smile.

"A hundred quid!" exploded Trevor.

"Fraid so" replied Beaky. "Ten loads at ten quid a load. It's the cost of the diesel for the tractor see, butty, but what you got to worry about? A hundred and fifty quid will be a drop in the ocean to what you're going to earn in the future."

Armed with the reassurance of Beaky, Trevor returned home to prepare his backyard to receive the mountains of manure that would raise his ailing fortunes. The following day dragged on with its usual monotony as he snipped away at the occasional customers' heads and at five thirty he eagerly locked the shop door in anticipation of inspecting his purchase at the rear of his premises. He rushed into the living room. Something was wrong. It was pitch black at five thirty in mid summer?

"That's strange." he said to himself. "It was broad daylight in the street just a minute ago."

He groped for the light switch of the darkened room to reveal the cause of the total eclipse of the sun: a hundred tons of chicken droppings. He rushed upstairs. It was halfway up the rear bedroom window. The whole of the backyard was immersed in a steaming mound of foul smelling chicken dung but worse still, the neat little brick built privy, that once stood as a monument of liberty and freedom, was now totally engulfed and inaccessible.

"I'll have to use the public convenience in the square," he mumbled with a sense of depleting resilience.

* * *

Without the slightest notion as to how he would process his hair-restorer, he began to draft an advert for the local press. "After forty years as a gents hairdresser," it read, "I have discovered the cure for baldness. Evans Hair Fertiliser will return your head to its former glory. See me in total confidence at my hair clinic, Forty Four Pant Street. Appointments unnecessary. Just join the queue."

Throughout the night Trevor experimented with the evil smelling dung retrieved by bucket from his rear bedroom window. He tried drying it into a powder that refused to adhere to his hairless head; he also soon realised that he might be reducing its natural hair growth properties as he cooked it in his frying pan.

"No. It's gotta be a paste, like," he murmured. "In its natural form, too."

By now his house was enveloped in an odious stench that began to infiltrate his entrepreneur's immunity.

"Got to do something about the smell" he said. "Aye. Bay Rum. That's the stuff. It'll put a bit of stay in it and make it smell better, like."

Each evening he mixed two buckets of droppings with a bottle of Bay Rum and the electric food blender turned the strange smelling concoction into a thick grey mass. He then packed it into an array of glass jars.

His advert in the Valley Times produced the desired effect and the morning following the publication a small queue assembled outside his shop.

"Come in, boys" said an elated Trevor. "If one of you will volunteer, I'll do a demonstration."

A completely hairless man stepped forward. He had the nickname of Alopecia Davies. Trevor frowned. He had known the man since school days and he could vouch that there was not a hair on his body from head to toe.

"Take a seat, then" he said, offering him the barber's chair. The screw top of the jar came off with a loud pop as the gas was released, and the audience grimaced as the shop was pervaded with a sickly odour of dung and Bay Rum. Trevor began to spread it all over the shining skin dome of Alopecia Davies.

"Just tell me what shape you want, boyo" said Trevor as he spread the rapidly hardening mixture enriched with builder's plaster.

"A Tony Curtis cut with a tapered back," replied an excited Alopecia and Trevor sculptured the paste an inch thick to resemble the head of the film star in the picture on the wall.

By the time thirty heads were released into the street wearing grey plaster helmets, a rumour quickly spread throughout the town that the German Army had come to Gilfach for mountain combat training.

24

* * *

Trevor had decided that the hair restoring helmets should remain on the heads for a month when the patient would return to the saloon for its removal, which was included in the charge of five pounds for the complete treatment.

The news of Trevor's miracle, whilst not proven, spread throughout the valleys, and even as far as Cardiff, to provide a constant stream of bald pilgrims in search of the elusive hair that he claimed to create. The atmosphere of Gilfach was electric as the day dawned that would reveal the scalp of Alopecia Davies and his thirty fellow guinea pigs to the world.

Trevor was awakened, as the early light of day entered his bedroom, by a rumble of voices in the street below. He quickly donned his jet black wig, the living proof, he had lied to his customers for the past month, that the magic elixir could return life to a dead head.

A pang of apprehensive fear hit him at the sight below where thirty grey domes were lined up for photographs by the media.

At nine o'clock he opened the door of his shop to be greeted by Alopecia Davies who seated himself in the barber's chair, followed by his companions who, along with the photographers, quickly filled the shop.

"Right then, boyos," said Trevor as he picked up a small hammer with a trembling hand and a nervous belch of wind. "Are you ready for the revelation, Alopecia?" "Aye," squeaked Alopecia.

The hammer struck the grey dome and a crack appeared followed by a low mumble from the audience.

"Are you all right, Butty? asked Trevor.

"My ears are ringing a bit," replied Alopecia, "but keep at it, boyo."

The hammer landed on the crack once more and to a loud gasp of spontaneous amazement the helmet split in two halves to fragment on the floor like a terracotta pot.

A stony silence of disbelief shrouded the room as Alopecia stared in horror at his reflection in the facing mirror. A golden down of young feathers covered his scalp.

"You've turned me into a bloody chicken," he screamed. "I'll be crowing and laying bloody eggs before long. Five quid for a head of feathers be damned. I could have bought a good wig for that money."

"Aye, an' where do you go for a haircut?" said another feather-headed client who had managed to remove his helmet. "A plucking machine, is it?"

An atmosphere of bedlam took over as Trevor's disgruntled customers removed their headdress to reveal fine crops of chicken down in various colours. They turned with menacing looks in his direction. He decided that discretion would be his prerogative in making a hasty retreat from the hostile crowd. He rushed to the rear door of his living room, completely forgetting the menace that lay beyond. As he turned the knob, a hundred tons of chicken manure swept through the building like a furious volcanic lava stream, taking all before it into the street.

26

Trevor was saved by the door that flattened him against the wall and, when the torrent subsided, he was able to escape via the rear lane. Nothing was heard of him for about two years, during which time his hated competitor, the young lady who ran the unisex salon in the square, was quick to add another service to her menu: feather plucking and styling. Then a postcard arrived at the Colliers Arms one day. It had the postmark of Auckland, New Zealand. On the reverse side was the photograph of a sheep-shearing gang. Trevor's short message read "That's me in the middle. Sorry about the mistake. Look me up if you ever come this way."

There was no address, of course.

CHAPTER
THREE

The Outing

Despite the fact that Gilfach Mawr lies in a saucer of hills at the head of the valley, it is served by a rail service. It also boasts an engine shed to house its single locomotive "Edith."

The normal service is to Pontypridd, where a connection can be made for the Capital City of Cardiff, but on special occasions, warranted by sufficient bookings, daily excursions are made during the summer months to such exotic locations as Barry Island and Porthcawl.

Oily Rag Evans is the driver, ably assisted by his fireman, Clinker Jones, and daily with the help of Edith they pull their two coaches to Ponty and push them back to Gilfach. With the exception of the odd incident, it is a mundane existence for the two men. The guard of the daily train is Back End Roberts, who constantly recharges his habitual thirst with a pint at the Station Arms in Gilfach and similarly at Ponty Station refreshment room. At the end of each day, as "Edith" steamed up the valley to Gilfach on her final trip, he lay prostrate in his guard's compartment, oblivious to all matters concerning the railway.

Always waiting at the engine shed was Clinker Jones's fiancée Bethan Jenkins. For years she had watched her lover shovel the dead fire and clinker from Edith's firebox.

"It's the miners' holiday next week," she shouted above the hissing steam and noisy ring of the fire-dropping shovel. "All the Karl Marx Club is going to Porthcawl, staying in caravans they are, like. D'you reckon we could have a week with 'em, like? We never been away together, have we?"

Clinker started to wipe his wet brow with a piece of cotton waste. "Never been away anywhere, never mind with you. The farthest I been is Ponty and Porthcawl." Bethan closed the firebox door to get her lover's attention.

"Why don't you broaden your horizons, Clinker? Gilfach, Ponty, Ponty, Gilfach and Porthcawl and Barry Island once a year. Other men in the town goes to Cardiff, and some have been to London, see."

Clinker began shovelling again.

"Well, 'ow the 'ell can I stay with you in Porthcawl for the week when I got to come back with Edith for the Ponty run?"

Bethan stamped the foot plate in temper, and jumped down.

"Well, bugger you, Clinker, I'm off home, an' don't forget my mother's coal tomorrow an' make it a big lump. The coal house is empty."

Bethan lived with her widowed mother in a railway cottage at the foot of a steep embankment just outside

29

of Gilfach Mawr, and it was a regular practice to roll a few lumps of coal from Edith to the cottage.

"If she wants a big lump, she can 'ave a big lump," said Clinker to his driver the following day as he prized a large boulder of coal from the bunker. "Must be all of two hundredweight," he gasped as he lined up the unintended missile in the doorway of the locomotive.

With years of attained skill Clinker took great pride in his marksmanship and the coal usually landed within inches of the coal house adjoining the cottage, but that day devotion to his loved one was tarnished from the previous day's argument and a devil-may-care attitude possessed him as he sent the coal on its perilous journey down the steep embankment. He looked backwards as Edith puffed on towards Pontypridd. The huge lump was heading straight for the cottage, straight for the front door, in fact. He was joined by Oily Rag, who often admired his precise aim, but he frowned as the huge black boulder careered towards the cottage.

"You've bloody well done it now, butty," he said to his terrified fireman. "She'll never speak to you again, that's for sure, init."

At that moment the neat front door with its polished brass knocker and letter box received the full destructive venom of the weekly coal delivery. It was torn from its lock and hinges as the coal made its forced entry into the living room, demolishing the age-old Welsh Dresser full of generations of priceless china-ware, before making an exit through the back door to destroy the outside privy.

With a merciful lurch, Edith took a bend and the horror of the destructive scene was obliterated. Clinker faced the boiler with an ashen tace as he pictured his ruined love life. On the return journey, after a stony silence for several miles, he spoke to his driver.

"You're right, mate. She won't talk to me again. She'll swear I done it on purpose like, in spite like for not going to Porthcawl with the Marx Club."

Oily grasped his mate's shoulder.

"You'll go to Porthcawl with her. It's your only chance, Clinker."

"But I can't, mate." replied Clinker. "I got no more holidays coming this year. I used em all up cockle picking, didn't I?"

That evening Bethan was waiting at the engine shed for her victim. Without the slightest consideration as to how he would do it Clinker jumped from the foot plate to comfort her.

"I've been thinking," he began before she could even start her well-rehearsed tirade. "I reckon I can make it to Porthcawl with you, like."

Her face mellowed into a smile. "An' you'll pay for a new front door, won't you?"

Clinker nodded his head in painful consent.

"An' all the crockery?" continued Bethan with a full victorious smile.

"Aye" murmured Clinker.

"Oh, an' the back door, my lovely," continued his rampaging fiancée. "It went right through, see. Didn't mess about like, did it, but don't worry about Mam, she's terribly shook up. She won't sue you for trauma and counselling like, but the Doctor says her nerves will come right with a couple of bottles of Guinness a day for the next year or so, ok, my lovely?"

Later that evening Clinker canvassed the regulars at the Colliers Arms in search of a potential fireman to take his place during the enforced holiday. His sole recruit was Delirium Davies, the drunkard of Gilfach Mawr.

"Why not?" he slurred. "Keep me off the booze for a week, won't it, like? Be like a holiday for me, not having to come here guzzling every day. Aye, I'll 'elp you out. What's in it for me though?"

"Half my wages," replied Clinker. "Seeing as you're not trained for the job."

The great day of the exodus to Porthcawl arrived in typical Gilfach climatic fashion as banks of drizzle rain engulfed the town. The local brass band tried vainly to play "We're all going on a summer holiday" as Edith steamed into the platform while leaving a trail of smoke and fire ash to enshroud her excited passengers.

"Do you think you got the hang of it?" asked Oily Rag of his confused fireman.

"I will after a few at the Station Arms to give me confidence like," replied Delirium Davies. "What time are we leaving?"

"You got twenty minutes," replied the worried driver.

On the platform Clinker glanced nervously at Delirium as he rushed past in his uniform to the oasis of the Station Arms, where he met the guard, Back End Roberts, already three pints in front of him.

Fifteen minutes later Edith's whistle advised them that it was time to leave. "

"Aw damn, I was just getting into the swing of things." said Delirium. "I tell you what, butty. You tell Oily that I've changed my mind like, will you?"

"You can't do that," replied the guard. "The bloody train won't go far without a fireman."

"Well, I'm not up to it really." said Delirium. "Clinker caught me out when I was drunk like an' I'd say yes to anything in that state."

The guard took his hat off.

"Here, swap hats. You be the guard an I'll do the firing. I used to be one before my eyesight failed."

"What 'ave I got to do?" asked Delirium.

"Just make sure all the doors are shut, then get in the guard's compartment, blow yer whistle and wave the green flag."

"'Right," said Delirium. "I can handle that."

Five minutes later Edith pulled out of Gilfach station full to capacity, and including Bethan and her lover bound for the delights of Porthcawl.

"Ten years I been waitin' for this moment," she said with dreamy eyes.

Two hours later the train arrived at Porthcawl.

"We'll uncouple here and go to the other end to take the train back to Gilfach," said Oily. "'Where the hell is Delirium?" he asked. "He should be here to do the coupling."

Little did they know that the temporary guard had suffered a change of heart as he blew his whistle and waved his green flag at Gilfach station. The call of the Station Arrns was too strong and as Edith slowly pulled the coaches away, he departed from the train to continue his true vocation, boozing!

Back at Porthcawl, as the train was made ready for its return journey to Gilfach, Back End the guard decided to search for Delirium.

"He must 'ave nipped off to the nearest pub as soon as we got here," he said to Oily with eager anticipation of an alcoholic recharge during his search. "I'll soon 'ave the bugger back here. We got ten minutes before we go, 'aven't we?"

Twenty minutes later the station master came up to Edith and her very worried driver. He carried his pocket watch in his hand.

"You should have been away ten minutes ago, driver," he said with his voice of authority. "Where's your guard?"

Oily fought for an excuse. "He . . . he got the wind bad, he 'ave an' he went to the pub, like, for some soda water, like, init."

The station master's eyes searched the foot plate.

"Well, where's your fireman?"

"I sent 'im to look for the guard," stammered Oily.

"Well, I suggest you go and look for the pair of them, because if this train is not away soon, I shall report the matter to the chief inspector."

By this time Back End was ten pubs and ten pints away from the station, in a futile search for a non-existent Delirium Jones, who was well and truly sloshed in Gilfach Mawr. Oily, who was a fairly temperate man, began his search and being of a modest nature, he thought it prudent to take a full half pint in each pub. He finally discovered Back End on his twentieth call as the guard collapsed at the bar and he did likewise, for the pair to be ejected into the road outside, by the landlord.

At that moment Clinker and Bethan were taking the sea air as they strolled hand in hand along the promenade.

"Bloody Hell!" shouted Clinker "What's those two doing here? They should have been on their way to Gilfach by now, like."

He knelt beside the two prostrate men. "What you doing here, boys?" he shouted as he shook each one in turn. Back End opened his glazed eyes and mumbled "Delirium went missing an' I been looking for 'im."

"Well, what's he doing here?" asked Clinker, pointing to Oily's prostrate form.

"Dunno," replied Back End. "Must 'ave come looking for me, I s'pose."

"Well, who's looking after Edith the train?" asked Clinker.

"No-one." gasped Back End. "You'd better take her back to Gilfach or we'll all 'ave the sack." And then he closed his eyes once more.

Clinker looked pleadingly at Bethan. "I know what you're thinking, but he's right. We'll all be for the high jump if we don't an' you won't want me without a job, will you?"

"But who's going to fire her?" asked Bethan.

"You are!" shouted Clinker, as they began to run for the station.

"Me?" shouted Bethan.

"Aye, you!" replied Clinker. "You've seen me do it long enough."

Later, as the soot-covered pair walked past the Marxist Club, it vibrated with raucous singsong.

"What's going on in there, then?" asked Clinker. "They're all in Porthcawl, ain't they?"

At that moment the Chairman staggered into the street.

"What you doing here, boyo?" he asked Clinker. "I thought you was having a week at Porthcawl, like?"

"'An' I thought you was too," replied Clinker.

"Well, we got a bit fed up, an' 'omesick like," answered the Chairman. "So we hired a few coaches to bring us up here on a mystery trip, like!"

CHAPTER
FOUR

The Yoga Class

Jones the Knot told me this story about himself, and he swears it's true.

It all began, he said, when he did his National Service in the forties. He was stationed in Germany, and during a night out with the boys in Berlin they decided to visit a tattoo parlour.

"She was a smart piece," said Jones. "A big blonde girl, like."

"Vot vould you like on your body?" she had asked. Jones avoided the obvious answer and shrugged his shoulders as his beer-glazed eyes feasted on her anatomy. "Vould you like 'Mudder' or somethin' like dat?" she suggested.

"Anything you like" replied the hypnotised Jones as he took out his cigarette packet. "I tell you what. You can print him on my chest" he said, pointing to the bearded seaman on the packet.

Four painful hours later, he raised himself from the couch to confront the mirror. His chest was totally emblazoned with a colourful portrait of a handsome bearded man.

"Where's his hat?" asked Jones.

"I decided to change him, and Zeus vould not look goot in a hat," she replied.

"What do you mean? Who the hell is Zeus, then?" asked Jones.

"Zeus was the god of all gods. No vomen gods could resist him."

Jones covered her artwork with his shirt. "Well, it won't do much for me up the valleys. There's no goddesses up there. That's for bloody sure."

Jones returned to Gilfach Mawr on his demob, but he found civilian life difficult to adapt to. He tried various jobs, but with a complete lack of any qualifications life proved extremely mundane to say the least. It was while he pushed his street-cleaning cart through Gilfach Mawr that he came across a little paperback book in a litter bin. *Learn Yoga* was the title.

During the following week he practised and perfected the various body-torturing postures while totally ignoring the delights of the Colliers Arms. Within three months he had reached the realisation of his path in life. He would become a yoga teacher; admittedly he did not have true qualifications, but who would know in Gilfach? He went down to Cardiff to an Asian shop who kitted him out in a flowing saffron robe and joss sticks of various odours. He grew his hair to shoulder length and soon he became a colourful character of the town with the obvious Welsh title of "Jones the Knot", the Guru of Gilfach.

He lorded over his congregation of leotard-clad females in all shapes and sizes as they transformed themselves into the shapes of his gentle commands. He burned his incense as they transcended in deep meditation while an air of total eastern tranquillity pervaded the corrugated iron community hall of Gilfach Mawr. He studied the passive faces of his clan. All female, with the exception of Acne Rees. "Blast him," he thought as he studied the small pigeon chested male of thirty whose youthful pimples had never left him. "Spoils the class he does. Only comes here to look at the women an' look at that silly smile on his face. He's enjoying himself wherever he transcends to."

His eyes continued along the rows of cross legged women, their hands held in the meditation posture, all with the feature of serenity on their faces. All except Esther Pugh, the noted feminist. Her sharp features remained as gaunt as ever. "I wonder where she transcends to," he thought. "Can't be the warm tropical beach that I send 'em to. It would have to be somewhere awful for men if she was to enjoy it. She hates anything with testicles, for that matter."

As he quietly recalled his class from their meditational fantasies, he noticed that they all gave lingering looks towards Acne Rees who smiled back at them. Of course, Esther Pugh remained aloof to the situation and gave Acne an acid glare that momentarily changed his smile to a look of stark fear.

The following week Jones the Knot decided to descend and meditate with his class after they had completed their postures.

"Compose yourselves, ladies," he said, totally ignoring Acne Rees who appeared to be eagerly anticipating the forthcoming experience. "We'll transcend to our own secret island, shall we?"

Rows of eager faces nodded their heads in agreement.

"Right then," began Jones. "Close your eyes and transcend. Imagine you are a falling feather gently zigzagging, down, down, down to a warm sandy beach. Just lay there in the sun and take in the sounds of the deep blue sea." As he spoke he conditioned his mind to take in his own instructions and soon he felt the pleasant experience of floating down towards the beautiful island of his imagination.

"What are you doing lazing on the beach, slave, when there is work to be done?"

It was Mavis Jenkins, one of his class members but dressed in ancient Roman attire.

"I'm not a slave, Mavis," he answered. "Don't you recognise me? I'm Idwal Jones, your yoga guru from Gilfach Mawr."

"Not down here," replied Mavis. "This is the Republic of Theodora and it's run by women. All men are slaves. Esther Pugh discovered it when she transcended and she's our queen. We follow her from your class once a week. It's great fun to be on top for a change."

Jones felt a sudden urge to return to his earth centre in the community hall but how could he recall himself now that he was part of the fantasy?

"Well, what about Acne Rees?" he asked. "He always returns from his meditation with a bloody great smile on his face."

"Well, he would," replied Mavis with a glazed look of passion in her eyes. "He's one of our pleasure slaves, you see."

"Is there any chance of me getting in on that?" asked Jones who fancied quite a number of his pupils.

"No way," replied Mavis. "Esther would never allow that because you have authority over us in the class and you must be subjugated in her eyes and not give pleasures like Acne Rees who is always meek in the class."

Their conversation was suddenly interrupted by the thunder of horses hooves as a twin-horse chariot raced towards them. The driver was Esther Pugh resplendent in Roman attire. She cracked her whip in temper at the sight of one of her subjects talking to a slave.

"Who is that malingering slave?" she demanded. "Do I know him?"

Mavis Jenkins stammered her reply in obvious fear of her queen, "He's Idwal Jones, our yoga teacher in the other world."

Esther put the tip of her whip under Idwal's chin to lift his face towards her.

"Ah! The guru of Gilfach," she said with a laugh. "You do realise that you are a trespasser in my world. A spy so to speak, and you know what we do with spies?"

Idwal began to feel decidedly uncomfortable in the presence of Esther, who could be a formidable character even in his yoga class, and his mind raced feverishly to think of a way back to his earth centre in the community hall. But who could recall him as he was now part of the fantasy? Esther blew a long note on her horn for several members of Idwal's class to appear in Roman military dress.

"Take him to the cells," she commanded. "I'll think later of his fate" and with that she lashed her horses to speed away across the sands.

Idwal was marched towards the town and placed in a cell beneath the public arena. There he found Acne Rees, who stared at him. "What the hell are you doing here?" he asked.

"Well, I'm not going to be as lucky as you from what I hear. That bossy old cow Esther Pugh is thinking of a fate for me."

"I wouldn't worry too much," replied Acne. "I know it seems a long time but we're only down here for twenty minutes until you recall us, like."

Idwal burst into an emotional tirade at Acne. "How can I recall you when I'm down here with you? You silly bugger."

Acne went pale. "Oh! Damn. I hadn't thought of that. Oh damn. That means we'll be down here for good. Oh damn. There'll be nothing of me left. Once a week with a couple of ladies is just fine but every day for good? Oh damn. That's too much of a good thing, like!"

Idwal consoled him with a pat on his shoulder. "Well, it's not that a bad way to go boyo. Lord knows what they got planned for me."

At that moment Esther Pugh appeared in the cell doorway. "Idwal," she said with her usual assertiveness. "I have decided to be reasonable with your fate. You will fight for your life in the arena tomorrow. Your competitor will be Brenda Evans."

"That's unfair," pleaded Idwal. "She's a bloody amazon is Brenda the Coal. I'm no match for her. She's become as strong as an ox on that coal round of hers. She slings bags of the stuff around like confetti."

Esther was immune to his pleading. "You'll be in the third bout tomorrow. Brenda will fight with dagger and trident and as a special act of mercy on my part you will be allowed to make faces at her when she attacks you."

"You do realise that if Brenda does me in, there's no chance of returning to Gilfach," replied Idwal.

"You can't pull that one on me" answered Esther. "You're not able to recall us and in any case I don't wish to go back to Gilfach with all you chauvinists. This is my paradise that I created so once you are destroyed there is no remote chance of our recall."

The following day saw Idwal in his flowing saffron robe standing on the sandy floor at the centre of the arena. It was similar to a scene from one of Cecil B. DeMille's Hollywood epics. He shielded his eyes from the intense sun as he looked up at his audience of women. Esther Pugh made a regal picture sitting in her royal box with the thumb of her right hand pointing down for the kill even before the one-sided bout had begun.

With a fanfare of trumpets Brenda Evans walked triumphantly into the arena, dressed in the full fighting armour of a Roman soldier. She bowed to the royal box and received a broad smile from Esther Pugh, who still had her thumb down for the kill. There was total silence followed by a spontaneous cry from the audience: "FOR THOSE ABOUT TO DIE WE SALUTE THEE!"

This did little to comfort Idwal's failing courage, considering his only weapon against this powerful warrior woman wielding a trident and dagger was to make faces at her. She began to approach Idwal, who started to contort his features, with little effect. Then she broke into a run, the six foot gentle coal woman in Gilfach but now his lethal assassin under the deadly spell of her queen, Esther Pugh.

Suddenly, as the female bore down on him in a death frenzy, he remembered his tattoo. Zeus the King of all Chauvinists. The god feared by all women. It might work on these Roman tarts all the same, he thought. With just twelve feet to go before Brenda closed on him, in desperation he tore off his robe to expose the colourful god on his chest. Brenda's look of elation changed to one of stark fear as she came to a halt. The whole arena fell silent, as she threw her weapons on to the sand before laying herself prostrate at Idwal's feet.

He walked slowly to the royal box where Esther Pugh surreptitiously moved her thumb to the upright position in a sign of clemency.

"You'll do more than that, woman," commanded Idwal in his strongest tone. "You'll pay homage to me. On your knees before me, I say."

In complete humiliation before her subjects, Esther sheepishly came down from the box. Then, quite suddenly, she was rubbing her eyes on the floor of the Gilfach Community Hall.

"All went to sleep, did you?" It was the voice of Police Sergeant Pritchard. "Do you know the time, man? It's nearly midnight. I saw the lights still on and decided to investigate."

Idwal was also rubbing his eyes, but with a broad smile of victory on his face as he confronted his confused and subjugated class.

CHAPTER
FIVE

Evans the Herbalist

The predominant surname in Gilfach Mawr is Evans, with fifty six in all. They were known by their profession, such as Evans the Milk, Evans the Bread, Evans the Undertaker, and Dai Evans, who was never without his binoculars, was referred to as Evans the Spy.

Evans the Herbalist was Chairman of the Council and was sometimes known as Evans the Godfather by Evans the Blue, the only Tory member at the town hall. Now Evans the Herbalist was an entrepreneur of the first degree with a finger in every lucrative pie of the town, whilst the innocent herbalist shop was partly a front to his more shady transactions under the respectable cover of the town council.

"I'm looking for some nice dressed stone," he said to Edwin Evans the town clerk as they chatted in the bar of the Colliers Arms following the usual weekly council meeting, when every proposal was passed except that of Evans the Blue.

The town clerk, generally known as Evans the Pen, tilted his trilby hat from behind, as he always did to shade his guilty eyes when a deal was afoot.

"It's hard to come by these days, like rocking horse manure, as they say. Got a little job, have you?"

Evans the Herbalist looked both ways in an act of secrecy before replying. "It's that bungalow I been building. I wanted to make a feature of the front in dressed stone, like."

"Oh," replied the Pen, trying to look naïve. "The thing is, dressed stone 'ave been dressed and built somewhere, like. So you got to pull something down to obtain it, like. If you see what I mean." Evans the Herbalist signalled with his eyes for the Pen to continue with the obvious forthcoming conspiracy. "You got to look for a building or a wall that would suit your purpose, and if that don't cause too much trouble, I'll put in a demolition order on the grounds that it's unsafe and an eyesore. See what I mean, like?" he said with a wink of his eye.

"What's it going to cost?" asked the Herbalist.

"Seventy five pounds consultant fees. Cash, if you please, like."

The two men shook hands and during the following week Evans the Herbalist scoured Gilfach Mawr for the elusive stone that would adorn his bungalow. His search proved futile and he was about to abandon his project in favour of a brick front to his new residence, when he emerged from the Karl Marx Working Mens Club one evening. It stood before him across the road with as much splendour as the Great Wall of China. Thirty feet long and ten feet high of beautifully dressed grey limestone.

"It don't serve any useful purpose," he mumbled to himself. "And it's a bloody eyesore come to that."

At the next council meeting it was proposed that the redundant wall be demolished as unsafe and a chain link fence be erected to replace it as a boundary for the rear gardens of Taff Street. With the sole habitual no vote from Evans the Blue, the motion was passed unanimously and a delighted Chairman of the Council paid his seventy five pieces of silver to the town clerk Judas.

W'thin two days the wall was gone but the little grey stone building that stood beneath its protective shadow for decades now exposed itself for the world to see. Etched in a marble slab was inscribed its glorious history.

> "THIS PUBLIC URINAL WAS ERECTED BY THE GILFACH MAWR URBAN DISTRICT COUNCIL TO COMMEMORATE THE RELIEF OF MAFEKING AS A SYMBOL OF FREEDOM TO ALL MANKIND."

The residents of Taff Street accepted the removal of the wall with little comment in the absence of Esther Pugh who was visiting her maiden aunt for a few days in the neighbouring valley. Meanwhile Evans the Herbalist wasted little time in completing the frontage of his bungalow and he hummed a tune of contentment. A week later he was arranging the final bottles of a pyramid of Evans's Elixir of Life in his shop window when suddenly the door exploded inward to send Evans into his meticulous display, scattering Elixir of Life in all directions.

"What have you done with my wall?"

Evans was about to realise the worst scenario of the wall conspiracy and he began to shake and itch with a nervous itch that only appeared in the face of dire fear. The tall gaunt woman of forty or so who faced him in her Harris Tweed suit was Esther Pugh, the dedicated man-hating spinster who lived at Forty Four Taff Street, the house that faced directly on to the nearby newly exposed urinal.

"I . . . I thought you would be along to see me," stammered Evans. "But after all, it was not your wall. It was the Council's, like, and besides it took the sun from your garden."

Esther ignored his excuses with a forced half smile. "And what have you done with the stone, Mr Evans?"

The Herbalist began to scratch violently as his itch of fear intensified. "I can't say to be sure," he answered. "Probably gone to the tip."

Esther folded her arms in a defiant gesture. "So that's what you call your fine new bungalow. A tip is it?"

Evans was now praying for the multi-arms of an Indian statue as his itch left no part of his body unaffected. "Well, I, er, sort of retrieved some of it after it have gone to the tip, like. If you see what I mean, like."

Esther continued to bait him. "I am a maiden lady, Mr Evans, and all my life that wall has shielded my innocent eyes from the debauchery and fornication of that disgusting urinal."

"But you can't see anything," pleaded Mr Evans. "It's nearly seven feet high."

"I can see the top of some men's heads," replied Esther "And to see the top of a man's head when he relieves himself is a downright obscenity to a lady like me."

"Would you like some free iron tonic for your nerves?" said Evans with a weak smile.

"There's nothing wrong with my nerves!" screamed Esther. "I want my wall back and if it's not replaced by this time next week the whole of Wales will know of your fraudulent behaviour."

She slammed the door behind her, causing an avalanche of Ginseng packets to bury the unfortunate Evans in his own window. That evening he called an extraordinary meeting of the planning committee. "It seems we have an anarchist in our community," he began. "The wall was removed with all the correct democratic procedures at our disposal and Miss Pugh is using the incident as an anti-feminist act on our part."

There followed a rumble of agreement from the totally male audience.

"Aye, an she'll be trying to get into our club 'fore long if we don't put a stop to it now," said Evans the Secretary.

"I propose a site meeting," said a member. "Half of us will go into the urinal and half of us in her house, and if we can't see nothing going on, then she got no case for us to answer, like."

It was decided to use the full council membership for the exercise with the ten men using the urinal to be

50

supplied with four free pints at the club across the road to make the act authentic. The whole assembly volunteered to a man for the urinal occupancy so lots were drawn for that enviable part of the experiment, with tall men being ineligible. Esther Pugh accepted the proposal under protest, saying that only the replacement of the wall would satisy her. The exercise was placed under the command of Councillor Jones in view of the fact that he could claim innocently of being a non-interested party by virtue of his name, which, of course, was not Evans.

With military precision, the following evening at six thirty he dispatched the ten lucky urinal actors into the Karl Marx Club, each with the price of four pints of beer. At seven o'clock their ten envious councillor colleagues assembled in Miss Pugh's bedroom to await the arrival of the urinal visitors. The atmosphere of the small bedroom became uncomfortably oppressive as the observers awaited the arrival of the imbibers from the social club, but as the time reached seven thirty, the urinal remained a quiet, solitary citadel, save for the occasional visitor, while the club across the road vibrated to a raucous chorus of Welsh rugby hymns.

"Go and shake em up, boyo," whispered Evans the Herbalist to one of his council minions as he tried to avoid the acid glare of Esther Pugh. Fifteen minutes later a motley procession of drunken councillors staggered across the road to the urinal, where they relieved themselves. They sang and they swore as any group of men will do in urinals, but they unknowingly played into the hands of Miss Pugh, who put on a horrified expression as the noise deafened everyone in the bedroom.

"I never heard that when the wall was there!" she screamed at the Chairman and the petrified town clerk.

"We're not here for a sound test, Miss Pugh," he stammered. "It's what you can see, like, and we can't see anything, can we?"

"That's not the point!" bellowed Miss Pugh above the din of singers. "I want my wall back!"

"Will brick do?" asked Evans the Herbalist in defeat.

"No!" shouted Miss Pugh, while stamping her foot in defiance. "I want the same stone that you stole for your bungalow or I shall expose you to all the Sunday papers and Gilfach Mawr will be disgraced nation-wide through your disgusting and obscene treatment of a gentle maiden lady."

The next evening Chairman Evans called an extraordinary extraordinary meeting where he was confronted by a very hostile crowd of his own party, but there was a deathly silence as Evans the Blue, the sole member of the Tory party, rose to speak.

"You realise that you are all guilty of fraud?" he began with the broadest of smiles. "Fortunately for me I was the only member to vote against this heinous conspiracy. A rose in the wilderness of evil, you might say, and if the wall is not replaced and Esther Pugh goes through with her threats of exposure, then I fear you are all for the nick."

There was an immediate uproar in the chamber.

"That's it, boys!" shouted one of the Chairman's ex-henchmen. "We'll work through the night. We'll pull the front of Evans the Herbalist's bungalow down and rebuild the wall as Esther Pugh demands, like."

"Not so fast, boys!" shouted Evans the Blue. "There's just one blue bottle fly in your ointment. Namely me. Even if the wall is then replaced, I want a reward for my silence in this very serious matter, like."

"What sort of reward was you thinking of, like?" asked the town clerk in a very subdued voice.

"I want to be in control for a change," replied Evans the Blue. "I'm fed up with being completely ignored all these years. Been treated like a leper I 'ave just 'cos I'm a Conservative!"

"But how can you be in charge, like?" asked the clerk. "You're only one, like, ain't you?"

"I'm well aware of that," replied the Blue, "but in future my vote will be the deciding vote."

"But that means we'll be a ship *without* a rudder, like," bleated a pathetic voice in the chamber.

"Precisely," answered the Blue. "I'm going to be your rudder an' I'll steer this council my way."

Total silence hung over the chamber as the members faced each other with helpless expressions.

"Well, that's it, boys," said the Chairman with a shrug of defeat. "He's got us beat an' if this gets out, we'll be the laughing stock of the valleys. A Labour Council with a bloody Tory Leader!"

Throughout the night they dismantled the Herbalist's bungalow by the light of car headlamps and during the day they rebuilt the wall while from the rear bedroom window of her house a delighted Esther Pugh watched them toil and a sexually contented Evans the Blue lay back on her bed.

Some weeks later the adjacent shop to Evans the Herbalist, that had been vacant for many months, was reopened. The windows were painted black and its title in gold leaf proclaimed it "The Private Shop."

"I don't exactly know what they sell there," answered the Herbalist to a prying customer, "but there's one down in Cardiff. A bit of a shady business if you ask me."

Later, when Evans closed the shop for lunch, curiosity got the better of him and he decided to enter the inner sanctum of the mysterious premises. The interior was low lit and, as his feet sunk in the thick pile carpet, his nose took in the strong sensuous smell of perfumed candles whilst low background music played romantic music. "Can I help you, sir?" asked the tall woman who confronted him. Her dress was as provocative as the atmosphere of the shop.

"Just having a look around," answered Evans, taken aback by the tone of her voice. He thought that he knew it but couldn't place it.

"We have everything here for the bedroom," she continued. "We even have a cream to soothe itching."

"Good Lord," exploded Evans. "It's Esther Pugh!" and he ran from the shop to the delight of Esther and her business partner Evans the Blue, who emerged from behind a curtain.

"That wall turned out to be a winner," he said as they embraced. "I'm now leader of the Council, and I passed planning permission to set you up in business here. No one objected at the meeting!"

CHAPTER
SIX

Fiddlers Two

Ossie Goldenberg, or Ossie Three Balls was the pawnbroker of Gilfach Mawr. A third generation valley boy who spoke with the same valley lilt as his neighbours, he could hardly be described as the Jewish Ethnic minority of the town. He often accused his arch rival in business transactions, Eli Jenkins, also a third generation valley boy of Cardigan descent, of being a Welsh Jew.

Eli was a wheeler dealer in any commodity, or any money-making scheme such as a house bug eradicator, that he sold in hundreds through press advertising. That particular venture came about when he acquired several lengths of three-inch square timber. He cut them into neat little blocks and marked each pair with Block A and Block B. With every pair he included a leaflet saying "FIRST CATCH YOUR BUG, THEN PLACE IT ON BLOCK A. FIRMLY COVER WITH BLOCK B. DEATH IS INSTANT AND CONFORMS TO ALL ANIMAL WELFARE REGULATIONS".

Ossie Three Balls was monitoring Eli's venture with great interest, and decided to embark himself into the direct lane sale of business, as Eli called it. "You wouldn't know where to start, Ossie." He told the pawnbroker in his shop one morning. "It's got to be legally illegal, if you know what I mean."

"Well, just you wait and see, boyo," replied Ossie. "My ancestors were dealing when you lot were still mumbling in your caves, like."

"Rubbish!" said Eli, storming from the shop. "I can make a few quid before you get out of bed in the morning. I could even tuck you up, an' you wouldn't know I've done it."

"That'll be the bloody day, boyo!" shouted Ossie. "That'll be the day!"

The following week Eli noticed a small ad in the *Valley Times*. It read "BANKRUPTCY STOCK OF TOP QUALITY CARPETS AT SENSATIONAL PRICES YOU WILL NOT BELIEVE. SEND £1 NOW FOR YOUR BOOK OF WONDERFUL SAMPLES."

"That's Ossie." he said to himself. "What's his game, I wonder?"

Much against his will Eli had to succumb to the temptation, and with great reluctance he forwarded his pound to a box number address for the mysterious book of samples. Within a week they arrived. Admittedly the twelve little squares were good quality, but the price list was ridiculously high.

"The cheapest is sixty quid a yard," said Eli aloud to himself. "What's his bloody game, I wonder?"

The following day he called on Ossie.

"What's yer game, boyo?" he asked the pawnbroker.

"What do you mean, butty?" said Ossie, trying hard to conceal a smile.

"Them carpet squares, and them daft prices, no silly bugger is going to pay that money, especially in Gilfach. I could carpet out a room for sixty quid, leave alone a bloody yard. What's your game, boyo? Come on, own up."

"You've answered yourself," said Ossie. "No-one in their right mind would pay that money, but even if they were daft enough, I would make a fortune on 'em, wouldn't I?"

"Well, what do you hope to make out of it?" insisted Eli.

"The samples," said Ossie. "The bloody samples. I don't really want anyone to buy the carpet. I'm making nearly a pound a time on the samples, see. I bought a load of off-cuts from Billy the carpet fitter, for a fiver. I cut them all into little squares an' I've sold 'em all for a pound a time, see. I've had a good response, too. Made about three hundred on the deal, beat that one. A far sight better than your bug eradicator, init?"

Eli's usual sarcastic response failed him. It was a magnificent piece of confidence trickery, far superior to anything that he had ever produced.

"Good one, Ossie," he eventually replied in humility and envy, as he sulked away from the shop in defeat.

A few weeks later a down at heel character confronted Ossie at his shop counter. His long unwashed hair reached the collar of his worn black velvet jacket, and his face carried several days growth of beard. He placed a battered old violin on the counter, and Ossie looked at it in contempt.

"What do you expect for that, then?" he asked. "It's knackered, init, like."

"It's part of me. It's my very life," began the pitiful man. "Do you know that violin has played in the best concert halls and opera houses in the world?"

"Well, what's it doing in bloody Gilfach?" asked Ossie.

"I lost it," replied the man.

"Well, you got it now," said Ossie. "So why don't you carry on playing in them posh places, like?"

"My ability, dear fellow," answered the man. "My ability to play this masterpiece, it departed from my soul overnight, and I was reduced to a street musician." He began to sob and brushed the sleeve of his coat across his eyes. "I'm afraid they do not appreciate the classics beyond the concert halls. It's this rock and roll music that they yearn for." He stared at Ossie with pleading eyes. "Could you trust me with a few pounds pledge for my lifelong friend? I need to eat to recuperate. Once I have regained my strength and dignity I shall find employment and repay you with the interest you desire."

For the first time in his life of pawnbroking Ossie was overcome with emotion and he shed a tear as he handed the man his pawn ticket and four pounds.

"One request," said the man as he was about to leave. "Would you be so kind as to place the violin in your window so that I can see it every evening? We have never been parted in forty years, you see."

"Certainly," answered Ossie. "I'll shove it right next to that ole accordion. It'll keep it company, like, won't it?"

Two days later a very distinguished gentleman came into the shop. He wore a large black snap brim trilby and a long scarf with one end wrapped around his neck before hanging over his shoulders on a long mohair overcoat.

"The violin in the window, my man," he said in a curt tone. "How much is it?"

"Can't sell it, I'm afraid," answered Ossie. "It's pledged for three weeks, like."

The man pulled off his kid gloves, ignoring Ossie's reply. "Can I see it, please?"

Ossie placed it on the counter. "You can look at it by all means, but he won't part with it, that's for sure. Comes here every night he does just to look at it in the window, like."

"I'm sure he does," said the man as he scrutinised the instrument thoughtfully. "Do you think he might accept an attractive offer?"

"How attractive might that be?" asked Ossie with a highly aroused interest.

"Five hundred pounds," snapped the man.

Ossie steadied himself by holding the counter. "I'll nab 'im tonight when he comes to look at it," he stammered. "But there's no guarantee that he'll accept your offer. He's played it all over the world, but he's in between jobs at the moment, a bit short of cash, like, init."

That evening he waited excitedly in the shop for his client to appear, and he tapped the window as the musician gazed longingly at his beloved violin.

"I'll 'ave a word with you, if you please," he said as he opened the door. "Come in a minute."

A look of fear came in the man's eyes. "There's still a few days left on my pledge isn't there?" he asked.

"Don't worry, my friend, don't worry," said Ossie with a consoling pat on his shoulder. "I had a man in here today an' he wants to buy it."

The man held his hand to his forehead. "Oh, I could never sell it, never."

"You will when you hear what he offered" said Ossie with a broad smile. "Fifty quid, what do you think of that?"

The man shook his head. "They offered me three hundred down at Cardiff when I was busking there last month." Ossie did a quick mental calculation and decided that a hundred and fifty pounds would be a nice profit.

"Well, he did tell me to start at fifty, like. What d'you say to three fifty?"

"No, no, I couldn't," replied the man in obvious mental anguish at refusing such a large sum.

"Four hundred," said Ossie with a much reduced hundred pounds profit in mind. "I got to be honest with you, that's the highest he will go, there's nothing in it for me 'cept my commission, like, init."

The man looked at the floor as his right foot played with the patterns of the lino and Ossie awaited his reply with hands clenching each other.

"Will it be cash?" asked the man. "I don't have a bank account."

"As you wish," answered Ossie while unlocking his cash box. "Just give me your pledge ticket an' here's your four hundred, like."

Ossie had been waiting a fortnight for the violin buyer to return, when Eli called in his shop.

"Sold that old violin, then?" he said with a broad smile. "What d'you get for it?"

"None of your bloody business," answered Ossie curtly. "But I'll make a handsome profit, that's for sure."

"You talking about that posh bloke, are you?" asked Eli.

"What do you know about 'im, then?"

"He's a Cardiff con man," answered Eli. "Disguises himself as a down an' out as well. Been working all the valley pawnshops, got a van load of old worthless violins, he 'ave."

Ossie suddenly turned white. "D'you mean to say I won't see 'im again?" he asked.

"No bloody chance," said Eli. "I tell you what, though, I'll take that old violin off your hands. What d'you want for it?"

"A tenner," replied Ossie.

"But you only gave four for it."

"How d'you know that?" asked Ossie with suspicion.

"Cos I was the conman who flogged it to you, an' one thing's for sure, I won't be the toff who'll buy it back at five hundred. Here's eight quid. You can double your money. I can make my next kill, boyo."

CHAPTER
SEVEN

A Gift from Heaven

Blodwyn the mare stopped obediently outside the Colliers Arms to allow "Scrappy" Jenkins his midday tipple.

"Not today, ole girl," he murmured from his cart as he looked behind to his collection of scrap iron: One clothes mangle, two sheets of corrugated iron and a baby's pram. "No. You got good intentions but that lot won't even raise the price of a pint. On you go, girl."

Later that day he arrived at his cottage and scrapyard on the common with only the addition of a few old saucepans to his miserable load, to be greeted by his wife Bessie from the doorway. Being a woman of considerable size, she filled the aperture as she began her usual tirade with a mixture of hearty laughter that caused her large bust to vibrate like blancmange beneath her printed cotton pinafore.

"They'll be waiting for that lot down the steel works. Must be worth all of fifty pence, that's for sure."

"That's enough of that sarcasm," Scrappy responded. "This trade 'ave 'ad it. Everything is plastic these days. No decent scrap metal about. I got to look for something else, like."

Bessie's face took on a more serious expression. "You said that about the salt and vinegar round, the firewood round and the cockles and laver bread round. You know what your trouble is, Enos? You don't go to chapel. That's your trouble. Your place of worship is the Colliers. How do you expect the Lord to find you there?"

Scrappy took his wife's rebuke like a guilty child as his left foot played with the loose gravel covering of the yard. He was totally immune to her outbursts as his mind conjured a collaboration with a reward in mind.

"Awright, Bessie. Awright. I'll go with you to Ebenezer chapel on a trial visit, an' if I like it, then I'll go regular, like."

Bessie rushed from the doorway to embrace him

"Oh Enos, my lovely! You're going to be reformed, I know it. You're going to join the flock!"

"Just a minute. Just a minute," replied Enos in a muffled tone as his face was pressed against her bosom. "I got one condition. A sort of last wish before I give myself to the church."

"Anything you like, my lovely," said an elated Bessie.

"Well, it's the darts finals tonight," replied Enos, "an' I'm broke, so could you lend me a couple of quid, like?"

Bessie gave him a push that sent him reeling back across the yard.

"You conniving old devil, Enos! Playing your evil tricks right to the end, but this will be the end. You'll go to chapel this Sunday if I have to drag you there, and you know I'm quite capable of that too."

"You don't sound very Christian-like to me," replied Enos as he raised himself from the floor of the yard. "I thought Christians were all kind and caring an all sort of gentle and quiet, like."

"Not when we're dealing with heathens such as you," screamed Elessie. "We have to fight with all our might. That's why we call ourselves Christian soldiers."

She went into the house to collect her purse from behind the mantlepiece clock before confronting her nervous spouse once more.

"Here! Take your wages of sin," she said, throwing him some coins which he quickly collected. "But make sure you pray for forgiveness next Sunday or woe betide you."

Enos was not himself that night in the Colliers and his score was the lowest of the team.

"What's the matter with you, butty?" asked Enquiring Evans, the local gossipmonger.

"It's my missus," answered Enos. "She's making me join the chapel."

"Never!" exploded Enquiring Evans at the top of his voice, shocking the Colliers into total silence.

"Aye, she's blackmailed me into it. I wouldn't be here if she hadn't lent me my beer money. Now I got to repay her by going to bloody chapel."

"She can't do that, boyo," protested Evans. "It'll turn your head, like, won't it?"

A rumble of agreement brought the bar back to life.

"I tell you what," said a self-appointed spokesman. "Why don't we all go to chapel with him to give him moral support, like, or he'll be out numbered else, won't he."

"Steady on. Steady on," said a lone voice from behind the bar. This was Crevice Hughes, the landlord. "What about me? The bloody pub will be empty, mind."

"Don't worry, Crevice," said a customer. "We'll make up for lost time when we get back. Might even be a lot thirstier after all that singing, like."

Ebenezer Chapel is a fine stone building at the very top of Pant Street, a steep hill with a gradient of one in six according to the sign at the bottom. People who climbed it regularly swear it was named because of the breathless panting it created and not for its true Welsh meaning. Forty-eight non-regular climbers from the Colliers Arms suffered great difficulty in reaching its summit on the Sunday of Scrappy Evans's indoctrination, and Ebenezer Chapel was stunned into silence as they filled the pews. Bessie Evans thumped her elbow into her husband's ribs.

"What's the meaning of this?" she hissed. "Are they all going to sign the pledge?"

"Only came to see I get fair play, like," answered Scrappy meekly.

"Anyone would think this is a court case instead of a chapel service," replied Bessie. "Now pull yourself together and pray for a bit of decent scrap to come your way."

Sleep eluded Scrappy that night. It came and went in restless spasms of fantasy as Crevice Hughes read the sermon from the bar of the Colliers Arms and the minister of the chapel served pints from the pulpit. Suddenly the deep silence of the night was disturbed by a whining roar terminating in a heavy impact that shook the cottage with the power of an earthquake. Scrappy rushed to the window followed closely by his wife. In the centre of the yard stood a strange object some twenty feet high. From its base came a fluorescent glow that cast a ghostly green light over its superstructure.

"It's . . . it's one of them flying saucers!" stammered Scrappy. "We're being invaded! I'd better get down the Colliers an' tell em."

But Bessie had been studying the wording on the object's body. It read: USA, N.A.S.A. SPACE MODULE TWO. She immediately began to concoct a plan to reform the wayward spouse in the most convincing manner possible.

"It's not a flying saucer," she said with her arms folded. "And if it was, the Collier's would not be open. It's four in the morning."

"Well, what is it then?" asked Scrappy nervously. "There's words on it. Tell me what it says, Bess. You know I am no good with words, like."

Bessie composed herself into a serene posture as she faced her trembling husband. "Enos, my loved one," she began. "You have been reformed. Out there is about thirty tons of best scrap aluminium."

"I know that. I can see that!" replied Enos excitedly. "But how do you know I'm reformed?"

"Because of the message," answered Bessie. "It says 'A gift from above'. Now who else would have sent it?"

CHAPTER
EIGHT

Troubled Waters

The Gilfach Mawr Sea Angling Club were having their Annual General Meeting in the spare room of the Karl Marx Social Club.

"Any questions?" asked the Chairman, Johna Davies, as he finished the reading of the Minutes.

"Is there any chance of us doing a bit more of sea fishing for a change, like?" replied the meek voice of Enos Lewis. "We bin formed for ten years now an' we aven't been to the sea yet."

"Well now," replied the Chairman, with contempt for the small man. "Apart from having no patience, the virtue of every fisherman, you got no bloody brains, Enos. We're forty miles from the coast, man, an' we never had any intention to go sea fishing in the first place. It was just a posh name we were after. How could we be expected to call ourselves the Gilfach Mawr Colliery Sludge Stream Angling Society?"

But this response to the small man's question caused a rumble of dissent among the six members present, who were also eager to try their luck on the shores of South Wales.

"What the hell 'ave got into you?" shouted the Chairman above the chorus of voices. "What's all this urge to fish all of a sudden? We were formed as a social club if you remember, to 'ave the weekly booze-up away from our wives, like, now you all got fishing on the brain."

"Well, I put it to the vote," shouted the Secretary. "Hands up all those in favour of a sea fishing trip."

Only the Chairman objected and the vote was carried.

"Seeing as how we don't know where to fish," said the Secretary. "I propose that we hire a boat and a captain like. They know all the best spots."

Two weeks later the Chairman called a further meeting of the dubious angling club.

"You'll be pleased to know I have found a boat and captain," he began, to a murmur of approval. "But there's a hitch, boys. He charges ten pounds per person per trip and he won't sail with less than twelve anglers, unless of course, we make up the cost." This time a murmur of disapproval came from the audience. "That means we pay up or find another firm like," continued the Chairman. "So I propose that we look for five more anglers. It's going to be expensive enough by the time we buy our bait an' beer an' not counting the cost of the bus fare down to Cardiff and back."

But the angling club discovered that the residents of Gilfach Mawr were quite reluctant to go to sea, and were soon reduced to enlisting lower members of the social scale in their quest. It took a fortnight to induce four dubious characters, leaving one vacant space, when Evans the Milk rushed excitedly into the Collier's Arms one evening.

"I've got him, boys! Israel Jones, the Bible preacher."

Johna Davies brought his clenched fist down on the bar counter. "Well, that just about caps it all, boys. What a crowd of bloody misfits to go fishing with. We got Ganja Evans the drug addict, Nancy Boy Adams the queer, Idris Morgan the undertaker, Sauntering Sid Lewis the tramp, and at the bottom of the barrel, Israel Jones."

"Oh, and there's a little problem with Israel," added Evans. "He won't come without his sandwich board."

"We're going fishing, for gawd's sake," replied the chairman. "In the middle of the Bristol Channel. Who the hell is going to read his bloody doomsday message out there?"

"Well, he won't go without it," said Evans. "He reckons as well as giving him faith in the high seas, it will keep him dry if it rains."

The following Saturday, they all assembled in the square for their journey to the coast.

"Down with the demon drink!" shouted Israel Jones as twelve cases of beer were loaded onto the bus, and as it left the square, his strong voice deafened the fellow passengers with the hymn "For Those in Peril on the Sea". At Cardiff Wharf they were met by an elderly man with a typical seaman's rolling gait as he walked towards them, but with a breath like a brewery. It was obvious that the sea was not the only thing that had induced his roll.

"A couple of rules before we start," he slurred, casting his thumb over his shoulder to a sickly looking craft. "She's got a slight leak, so you take it in turns on the pump. Awright, our kid? And secondly, there'll be no heavy feet on the deck 'cos she's got a ripe plank here and there."

The twelve men boarded the vessel on tiptoes with their faces tense with trepidation as Israel Jones quoted a psalm of impending doom. The captain started the engine with jump leads to the battery of an aged Morris Minor on the quayside and ten minutes later they began to feel the swell of a not too hospitable Bristol Channel as they prepared to reap the harvest of the sea.

The trouble began when Ganja Evans, after a few bottles of beer, began to feel generous with his roll-ups of marijuana. Soon, with the exception of Israel Jones, the whole ship's complement were totally inebriated with a cocktail of beer and ganja. The pumping task was completely ignored and all thoughts of fishing was forgotten as the vessel slowly sank lower into the sea and Israel Jones paced the deck in his sandwich board, condemning the raucous passengers and captain for their evil ways.

Ten thousand feet above them another drama was taking place. A passenger aircraft en route from London to New York had to make an emergency landing, and ten tons of fuel were jettisoned for safety reasons. It began its descent along the Bristol Channel with the atomised cloud of high octane vapour landing harmlessly on the water below, but right in its volatile path was a slowly sinking fishing boat.

"Come on, have a drag of the happy weed, you miserable old bugger," taunted Ganja Evans to Israel Jones.

"Tempt me not!" shouted Israel, throwing his clenched fists to the sky. "Hellfire and brimstone will descend upon you all for your sins!" And as he finished his damnation, so did Ganja strike a match to light a fresh roll-up. At that very moment the tip of a ten-mile long trail of fuel reached the burning match and, with a roar like that of a jet engine, the whole area became enveloped momentarily in a brilliant flame that shot away to the heavens before the astonished eyes of a singed and bewildered ship's complement.

"It worked! It worked!" shouted Israel. "I knew it would! Now, you Sinners, behold the power of the heavens above. On your knees to seek forgiveness!"

A new corrugated iron church has been built in Gilfach Mawr. The congregation consists solely of the passengers and captain of that ill-fated fishing boat that was struck by the Wrath of God for their sinful behaviour, and every Saturday they can be seen parading the square in their sandwich boards, led by their pastor, the Rev Israel Jones.

CHAPTER
NINE

The Tiger-Man of Gilfach

Many years ago the Italians invaded South Wales. Restauranteurs they were, and before long their coffee machines screamed in discord throughout the valleys. Not a word could be heard in their well-stocked cafés as the scalding steam pipe gurgled into the ice cold milk and the tenor voices of the operators rendered forth Verdi arias.

Most invasions, however, produce a cross-fertilisation of culture and Guiseppi Franchiano achieved just that, earning undying gratitude from the people of Gilfach Mawr, when he invented his pie-warming saucepan. Until then the humble meat pie was eaten cold, or warmed in the small gas oven beneath the counter to produce a hard crab-like shell with a small kernel of dried meat at its centre. Guiseppi's saucepan was tailor-made to take one pie. It had a hinged lid with a hole in the centre. Through the hole right to the middle of the pie ran the steam pipe of ornate counter boiler. With a turn of the valve, the trapped pie gave a series of deep death rattles as the scalding steam converted it into succulent image of a glorious flexible steak and kidney pudding.

With a flourish and an aria, Guiseppi would squelch it onto a plate, to be smothered in brown sauce from the flagon on the counter. No other meal in the history of Welsh cuisine, be it leeks, laverbread or faggots and peas, could better it. There were traditionalists who complained that the coffee tasted queer after the pipe had served a pie, but Guiseppi patented the saucepan and became rich and famous overnight. Now the firm entrusted to make the famous appliance was the Aberboi Tin and Wire Company in the next valley.

Their main output came from the manufacture of wire-netting, saucepans and mousetraps, and during Guiseppi's frequent calls at the factory, he fell for the dark Celtic eyes of Minerva Evans.

She was a mousetrap assembler and with a name like Minerva, Welsh wit ordained her "Minnie Mouse". But Guiseppi was never to be her lawful Mickey. The South Wales Mafia would permit no intrusion of Celtic blood into their Neapolitan lineage. However, Minerva became pregnant and later gave birth to Luigi — Luigi Caruso Evans. The Christian names were a form of insurance for the father's maintenance money, whilst the surname was a defiant gesture of the proud Minerva that she remained Welsh.

Five years later Guiseppi died, leaving his café to Minerva and the patent of the pie-warmer to Luigi. The boy grew up into a valley lay-about on the constant proceeds of his father's invention. Dressed in his regular garb of a dark pinstripe double-breasted

73

suit, patent leather two-tone black and white shoes, black tie, white shirt and a snap brim trilby, he was known as "The Godfather" to the members of the Temperance Billiard Hall where he passed most of his life.

Progress however took its toll and the patent pie warmer was superseded by the high speed microwave oven. Admittedly the succulent dollop of oozing pie prepared by the simple little saucepan was far superior to the offering of its electronic counterpart, but the busy valley people welcomed the advent of the high speed pie and the little saucepan was put to rest.

Luigi then preyed on his mother's resources until she was forced to place an embargo on his finances and the stark reality of work finally loomed before him in the shape of the Gilfach Mawr pithead. He stopped at the working men's club to subdue his hysteria before committing himself to an alien life of manual labour.

"Not going to make a start, are you?" said the red-faced steward as he presented him with a pint of dark. "A bit late in life, I thought, like. Come 'ard to you, won't it, like?" He continued, "Wild 'orses wouldn't get me down there." He paused to swallow the remaining two-thirds of his pint. "'Pneume, pneume, damn, I can never say that word without my teeth, but it's dust you'll end up with down there, you mark my words."

After a further two pints and the continuous tirade of the steward, Luigi had decided against becoming a miner.

74

"You've convinced me," he said as he spun from the bar. "I'm going to make my fame and fortune elsewhere. Gilfach's too small for me."

"Where you going, then?" shouted the steward as Luigi neared the door.

"Abroad," replied the Celtic Neapolitan.

Five hours later the paddle steamer *Cardiff Queen* made fast at the pier of Weston-Super-Mare and the Welsh immigrant Luigi Evans proudly stepped onto English soil. His undoing, however, in the new-found land of opportunity was the pub at the end of the pier and the raven-haired beauty who served there. Like a Bristol Channel siren, she lured him on into drunken oblivion, only to leave him spreadeagled in the doorway after closing time.

"Duw, duw, mun," said a member of a group of Welsh people as they passed by to board the last steamer of the day. "I knows 'im, it's Luigi Evans, always 'angs around the Temperance 'e does."

"Well, let's take the poor blighter 'ome," said another. "'e 'aven't got a leg under 'im."

And so Luigi was returned to Gilfach. However, he was undaunted; the pioneering spirit within him was all powerful.

"I'll start nearer 'ome," he murmured to himself as he took practice shots in the Temperance. "Barry Island, like, there should be openings down there for a bloke like me."

The busy holiday resort on the edge of the Bristol Channel is the playground of the valleys, a day tripper's paradise if ever there was one, cocooned in a steaming odour of fairy floss, hot dogs, hamburgers, chips, toffee apples and cockles, the packed sandy beach resembles a population explosion far worse than the banks of the Ganges. Behind it the pleasure park roars on unabated with amplified pop against a background of noisy mechanical death-defying rides. It wasn't new to Luigi. At least once a year since the age of five he'd made the pilgrimage, yet he still walked between the shows with an awed expression.

A loudspeaker with a squeaky recorded address drew his attention.

"Is it human, or is it a spider? Come inside and see for yourself, Zarita the amazing Spider-Woman. We only charge to keep her in flies, but be warned, do not stand too close, and do not touch her, she's not impartial to human blood."

A trickle of people paid their entrance money to file through the gaudily painted spider web entrance. Luigi felt inquisitive. The large watery fat man who had been poured into the small cashier's office took his coins with a blank look.

"'Keep moving, please, and don't touch her," he repeated in utter boredom and Luigi came face to face with Zarita. She had a pleasant little face, for that was all one could see of her, set in the centre of eight synthetic hairy spider' legs. The lights were subdued, and shone onto a back-cloth of black drape. She smiled at Luigi, a forced smile, and then she changed to a relieved straight face, but Luigi stayed.

"I wish you'd move on," she hissed in a Birmingham accent. "There's other people waiting to see me."

Luigi glanced back at the entrance.

"No, there's not," he whispered. "There's only me, like."

Zarita gave a contemptuous nod of her head, causing her eight legs to quiver realistically on their fine wire suspension.

Luigi was enthralled. "Who made the get-up for you, then? Good, innit?"

Zarita was far from impressed with his interest. A fierce Spider-Woman chatting with her spectators was not the image the management desired.

"I'm having a break in ten minutes," she said nervously, "I'll see you outside and tell you all about the job, now get out of here or I'll have the sack."

The truth was that Luigi, with only a head to go on, had fallen for her. She met him near the cafe as promised. A petite young lady, and well-proportioned to match her pretty head. Luigi became even more impressed as his bulging eyes scanned the rest of her, minus the spider legs.

"Not from these parts, then," he said as he placed her coffee on the table.

"No, Brum," she answered. "I though I was going to make a name for myself on the stage, and the best I can do is a spider's head at Barry Island." She paused to start her drink. "I'll tell you what, though, there's a lot of money in these side shows. My boss runs a Rolls on 'em."

Luigi began to fantasise. He sat behind his massive desk in a penthouse office suite. On the glass door three secretaries away gold lettering read "Luigi Evans

Enterprises". His jewel-covered fingers strum on the phone as he ponders on a call to Disneyland. Zarita the Spider-Woman in a revealing Paris creation is draped along the chaise longue.

"Do you reckon you could take on the part of a Tiger-Man?" she asked, and the fantasy vanished. "You wears a tiger skin like, an' I does the speaking, all tarted up in a harem costume. There's a pitch going vacant on the ground."

Three weeks later, beneath a gaudily painted canopy depicting a savage tiger with a human face, Zarita carried out her well-rehearsed speech to a receptive audience of day trippers.

"Ladies and gentlemen, let me tell you the story of Kador. Fifteen years ago, on the slopes of the Upper Punjab, a group of women from my very own village were picking tea for Ty-Phoo when a massive Bengal tiger attacked them. He ate two, but the third one he raped. She survived to be taken back to the village where ten months later she gave birth to a tiger with a human head. For a time she suckled the creature, but he soon rejected the milk of her delicate breasts in favour of raw meat. Nothing could appease his appetite for blood, then one day as he played happily in the village with the other children, he ate one. The headman said 'He must be destroyed'. But I begged for his life and since then we have travelled the world together as man and wife. Come inside and see Kador the Tigerman, but be warned: he is savage, and he has never forgotten the taste of human blood, so please stand well back."

Inside, Luigi, dressed in the padded tiger skin walked nervously on all fours within the confined space of his small cage. Zarita entered, followed by her first audience. She rattled her cane along the bars.

"Ladies and gentlemen, although he is my husband, he has to be caged for your safety. He just cannot trust himself when he smells humans. Only I have the power to control him."

Luigi made a well-rehearsed growl at a boisterous youth who said he was "a bloke dressed up".

"Would you care to tell him that inside the cage?" said the show-woman Zarita. "It can be arranged as long as you sign one of our forms to absolve us from any injury or even death on your part." The youth scratched his worrying acne and sank back into the crowd.

That evening the two imposters counted their spoils.

"Better than ever I made on the pie saucepan," said Luigi. "Bloody hot, though."

Zarita was pensive.

"I got an idea after handling that mouthy kid today. I'll get some forms printed and offer a hundred pounds reward to anyone who'll enter your cage."

"Not on," said Luigi. "A big bloke might fancy his chance and hit seven sorts out of me."

"No fear of that," said the persuasive Zarita. "When you offer a hundred quid, that scares 'em, really makes 'em think there's something in it, like."

Luigi shook his head but Zarita would have her way. The following week a new addition appeared on Luigi's brightly painted publicity posters.

79

"KADOR THE TIGER-MAN NEEDS HUMANS.
 WOULD <u>YOU</u> DARE ENTER HIS CAGE IN
SACRIFICE OR AS A MODERN DAY GLADIATOR?
 THE MANAGEMENT WILL PAY A HUNDRED
POUNDS TO ANY BRAVE PERSON WHO
SURVIVES FIVE MINUTES IN THE CAGE OF THE
MIGHTY KADOR."

For most of the season the show flourished and no-one accepted the challenge, which had created a strong superiority complex within Luigi, making him a more authentic Tiger-Man. Zarita was the dominant character of the partnership and her future plans for a Camel-Man, a Crocodile-Man and even a Snake-Man, worried Luigi. He began to culture nostalgic dreams of the Temperance Billiard Hall in Gilfach Mawr as more attractive than writhing around Barry Island in a boa constrictor skin.

On the last Sunday of the season fate dealt a cruel blow to the enterprising couple. A group of ardent drinkers from the Gilfach Mawr working men's club had decided on an end of season booze-up at Barry Island. Many were members of the Twenty Pint section, and after they completed the ritual they headed for the fairground. By late afternoon the inebriated party arrived at the lair of the Tiger-Man, where Zarita beckoned them near.

"Come inside, boys, this is your last chance to see the savage Kador."

They needed little encouragement and soon Luigi was surrounded by twenty-five beer sodden valley boys. Their major spokesman was a giant of a man called Pitprop Parry, a name earned by breaking a prop in two with a karate chop. He was banned from playing with every rugby club in South Wales on humanitarian grounds. Luigi began to shake violently and made a vibrato roar as he recognised him.

"Don't look much of a man-eater to me," said Parry turning to Zarita. "Any advance on the hundred quid if I eat 'im, like."

She began to pale, and Luigi's tremor advanced into a convulsion which rattled every loose object throughout the tent.

"Where's the form then, love?" said Parry with a confident glance at his supporters.

"He's gone for bigger blokes than you," said Zarita as she offered him the document.

"Don't worry about me, love," replied Parry. "Just open his cage, like, and get the hundred quid ready."

Luigi began to panic as the giant entered his lair.

"Don't come any nearer, boyo, or I'll eat you," he stammered in a strong Welsh accent. Parry's shovel-like hand grabbed his skin by the neck to tear it completely from his body, revealing the trembling naked body of Luigi Evans the Gilfach Layabout.

"I knows 'im," said one of the crowd. "Plays snooker in the Temperance 'e does."

"Well, 'e won't no more," said Parry as he dangled Luigi's white, limp figure from his outstretched arm. "'cos I'm going to eat 'im."

With that the Tiger-Man gave a loud scream as Parry bit his ear.

"Give 'im the hundred quid!" he cried out to his ashen-faced partner. "Give 'im the money for gawd's sake or there'll be none of me left!"

That was the end of Luigi Evans's masquerade as the Tiger-Man, and his partnership with Zarita the Spider-Woman. Pitprop Parry became enchanted by her bewitching power and become Garth the Gorilla-Man at Barry Island.

And Luigi? Well, he has a job up at the electric factory, making microwave ovens.

CHAPTER TEN

The 'Ole and the 'Ill

Joshua Jenkins cried wolf for the last time during his eighty fifth year.

It was his habit to endorse any statement, true or false, with "May the Lord strike me dead if I'm talking a lie", and before a crowded audience at the Colliers Arms the Lord finally took him at his word.

Joshua often boasted that he was a land owner of no mean size. When questioned as to its location, he would reply "Australia, mun, that's the place to live, goes on an' on as far as the eye can see", and you were left to muse on a clever evasion. His boundless area of down under was actually at the end of a neat little street of terraced houses on the edge of a grass common in Gilfach Mawr, ten acres in all but, but the contrast to the wide-open spaces of Australia was extreme to say the least: rather undulating, they consisted of a slag heap and a quarry, two ghostly citadels of a bygone era of open mining. Joshua had paid fifty pounds for the site when he was an ambitious young man of twenty five. "I'll make something great out of those two one of these days," he would tell his young wife when she queried the squandering of their complete savings.

The since departed Mrs. Jenkins spent her lifetime listening with Victorian obedience to Joshua's plans for the 'ill and the 'ole as he called his property. The schemes were usually disclosed after a night at the Colliers, when expense was of little concern. They included such mammoth concepts as converting the quarry into a lido and the slagheap into a ski centre, but the following day a more sober mind would reject the plan as being perhaps a little too far reaching for the eighty inhabitants of Gilfach.

There was an air of expectation and prosperity as Joshua's will was read out by the junior member of Bradworthy, Jones and Sopworth in their office at Pontypridd. The two middle-aged men facing the solicitor passed more than a look of dissent at each other. It was no secret that they had not spoken in thirty years for a small quarrel had turned into an irreversible feud, and whilst their two families faced each other across the street of the quarry and the slagheap, never a word passed between them, man, wife, son nor daughter. The situation had stabbed like a thorn into Joshua's lighthearted way of life, and right to his death he sought to remove it by playing the mediator, but the knot of hatred was too strong even for him to sever.

"My property known as Jenkins Investment Holdings Gilfach 1920 Limited," read the young solicitor, "shall be divided between my two surviving sons as follows. Project number one, the quarry, to my son Owen. Project number two, the slagheap, to my son Isaac."

84

Owen, the elder of the two sons, screwed his rolled cap until his knuckles whitened. "That's it then, is it, Mr. Sopworth, the 'ole for me and the 'ill for 'im?"

The solicitor peered over the top of his half spectacles. "There only remains your father's personal effects and the contents of the rented property known as thirty six Quarry Street. All of no great value, but nevertheless to be shared between you and your brother".

The two men rose to leave.

"Just a moment, gentlemen," said the solicitor. "Your father confided that he suffered many years of torment and grief over your, er, your quarrel. As he was unable to bring you together during his life, he has sought to do so in his death".

Joshua's sons leaned forward eagerly only to return to a contemptuous slouch as the lawyer read the terminal clause of the will.

"The property, gentlemen, the quarry, and the slagheap. There shall be no individual development or sale of these items without the consent of each of you." The solicitor smiled his unamused professional smile. "Your father's logic is that the Hill and the Hole shall be a bond, a bond that may one day mature into a sound renewal of your friendship."

* * *

For three long years the feud continued whilst the shining slag of the hill nurtured its sparse buddleia bushes, and the quarry received two prams, four beds and a bicycle within its algae-covered water.

One cold November Sunday, Owen braced himself to look down on his property, unaware that his brother was less than a few hundred yards away, shading his eyes against a winter sun as he studied the black peak of his bequest. Scarcely a Sunday had passed since Joshua's death that the two men had not made their compulsive pilgrimage to the Hill and the Hole. Both would leave by their rear entrances to arrive at their individual shrines of meditation with a mixture of contempt and nostalgia for their father.

Owen mumbled into the sharp wind "Bloody 'ole. Other sons, they gets left 'ouses or a bit of money, but not Joshua, no, he leaves me this, a dirty big festering 'ole."

As if to echo his feelings, Isaac's lips moved in silence as he thought his thoughts. "I'll bet you're up there laughing at me, dad, sat right on top of your precious 'ill so's you can keep an eye on your precious 'ole."

That evening a large car with a cherished registration purred to a stop at the home of Owen whilst the curtains of Isaac's house moved with the speed of semaphore flags. The night intruder of the quiet street edged his way between the piano and dining table of Owen's furniture-crammed parlour.

"My card, Mr. Jenkins. Levy is the name, Harold Levy of Quickbuild Developments Limited." He paused to offer cigarettes without success. "I am interested in the purchase of your quarry, Mr. Jenkins."

Owen pointed at the window. "Can't do nothing without 'im agreeing over there an' he can't sell without me. It's all in the will, see."

The developer closed his briefcase. "I am aware of your little quarrel, Mr. Jenkins, but all I need is signatures. You need never utter a word to each other."

* * *

Two years later the towering slagheap had relinquished its vigil over Quarry Street to nestle, with the aid of an army of bulldozers, into the welcome bosom of its friend the quarry. On the now level ten acres stands the Joshua Jenkins housing estate, and whilst that gentleman's sons only greet each other with a "say cheese smile" as they tend the gardens of their newly built houses, the feud is really over, and Joshua looks down with pride on his legacy and his wisdom.

CHAPTER
ELEVEN

Idwal The Terrorist

Idwal James' trouble with life was progress: the lack of it, that is. When his father lay on his deathbed on a cold November day in 1966, he said, "Idwal, when I go, boyo, let the old bus go with me. She's too old, she've 'ad enough. Keep up with the times, gimme a cheap burial, just the 'earse like, an' put the rest of my insurance as a deposit on a posh new coach."

But Idwal had other plans for the death benefit of his father. The money would go to the only passion in his solitary batchelor life: Fish. The little corrugated iron bungalow on Gilfach Common boasted no less than five aquariums plus two garden ponds well stocked with golden carp and Japanese Koi.

On the day of the insurance payout, Idwal stood in the nearby garage, where lived the veteran bus that rarely left the confines of Gilfach, being mainly employed on school service, her only means of revenue. He patted the brass radiator top of the ancient charabanc with her convertible canvas hood.

"Plenty of years in you yet, old girl, an' a bit of character, more than you can say about them new fangled things. A marine aquarium, that's what I'll 'ave," murmured Idwal. "Aye, a tropical marine layout in the 'ole man's bedroom," and the bus seemed to wink her brass headlamps in approval.

That evening the secretary of the Workmen's Hall called at the bungalow. Idwal spoke to him through a quarter opened door.

"What can I do for you, Mr Watkins, then, you've come at an awkward time. Just feeding the fish I was."

"Well, don't treat me like a mugger, Idwal, you knows who I am, so let me in then."

"Never know, mun," said Idwal. "I got some valuable fish here, I 'ave."

Once inside, the secretary wished he'd stayed at the door as five aquarium air pumps gurgled relentlessly.

"What d'you say to a trip to Cardiff, then, Idwal my boy?" he shouted above the din.

"Cardiff?" stammered Idwal. "I only been there once, Mr Watkins, with my father before the war when the bus was in her prime like, don't know how she'd take to it now like."

The secretary strummed the hard dome of his bowler with nervous fingers. The truth was that he'd forgotten to book a coach for the International rugby match at Cardiff and Idwal's museum piece was his last resort.

* * *

The following Saturday saw a nervous charabanc driver take his vehicle over the common cattle grid in the direction of Cardiff as the twenty noisy passengers rendered *Calon Lan* in complete discord. Idwal, however, had come prepared with the aid of industrial ear protectors, despite their alien appearance in combination with his cloth cap and belted raincoat. Three hours later as the tired bus steamed to a welcome halt at the sacred Arms Park, Idwal's utterly inebriated passengers fell down its rear steps to head for the nearest pub.

The spectacle was eagerly applauded by hundreds of rosetted supporters who accepted the antiquated mode of transport as a pageant of the golden past. Idwal was unconcerned as he unfastened his enamel licence from his lapel before taking in the delights of the capital. Now right in the city centre, beneath a statue of John Batchelor, whoever he might be, are underground toilets. Well-kept ornate affairs they are, with gleaming copper and brass fittings to adorn shiny white porcelain and marble surround. Idwal took his relieving position in the long row of curved stalls as the automatic cisterns sang their watery little tunes in preparation for their next douche.

His eyes travelled *slowly* up the sparkling copper pipe to the cistern tank. It was large with glass panels. Just like an aquarium, he thought. Was he dreaming? Had the Journey from Gilfach been too demanding? There were fish in it, one, two, three, four, five golden carp, beauties too.

Suddenly the tank began to flush. "Genocide!" screamed Idwal. He gripped the sides of the closet in stark terror as the water level dropped and the five carp dived for the security of the remaining water.

No one took the slightest notice of his hysterical outburst as his wild eyes remained transfixed on the diminishing water. Suddenly it stopped with a definite thump, leaving precious little depth for the fish as their dorsal fins became exposed.

"Carnage!" screamed Idwal.

"Wino having a turn," said the occupant of the next closet.

Then the ballcock began to refill the tank and the grateful occupants began to rise.

"Look at their eyes!" shouted Idwal. "Full of stark terror they are."

"I'll 'ave to ask you to leave my convenience, our kid," said a little man at his rear, wearing a very official peaked hat. "Them carp is the best fed in Cardiff," he continued in a strong Cardiffian accent.

"But they gets their brains bashed in about sixty times a day according to my reckoning," shouted the emotional Idwal.

"Now look 'ere, kiddo," said the attendant. "We 'aves all sorts of weirdos down 'ere, so please adjust your dress as the notice says and on your way, right."

Idwal gave the man a contemptuous glare as he made for the street above and the outstretched arms of John Batchelor, wearing a traffic cone on his head and resembling a leprechaun more than the philanthropist of his title.

As the day wore on and the triumphant roars of approval for Welsh tries only vibrated over the capital, Idwal returned to the fish many times. The attendant was immune to the activities of weirdos, winos, flashers and fish fanciers, as he sat glued to his transistor bringing the latest result from Arms Park. Idwal made notes and drawings in a newly purchased school exercise book.

As he nursed his bus back to Gilfach, this time without ear protectors, there was a distinct expression of satisfaction on his face. Six weeks later he sold up, lock, stock and barrel. The bus went to the Ancient Vehicle Society, the fish and aquariums to a pet shop in Pontypridd, the bungalow was bought by a local farmer for use as a chicken shed, but no-one would buy the contents. There was eventually a compromise with the organizers of War on Want, who took it away for a fee of twenty pounds. The day of the next home international dawned at Cardiff, and France were the visitors. Idwal took a service bus to the capital disguised as a Welsh supporter with a large leek, rosette, scarf and rattle.

Now the area that John Batchelor surveys from his lofty plinth is French in appearance. An open air café sits near the subway to the toilets surrounded by mature trees where the patrons supped their beverages and watched the world go by. But that day the atmosphere was truly Parisian — with a predominantly French patronage. The air was strong with Gitanes and garlic, and the familiar Cardiff brogue was non-existent.

Carrying a large holdall, Idwal began his descent to the toilets half an hour before the kick off. He was lucky. Just three sets of feet showed beneath the locked doors of the W.C. The attendant was busy preparing his small office for the match as he removed his peaked hat, switched on his transistor and poured a glass of beer. And that was the sum total of Idwal's hostages! Zipping open the holdall, he produced a near perfect model of an automatic machine gun, four plastic hand grenades and a velvet bag to cover his head.

The attendant was oblivious to the noise as Idwal closed and bolted the outer door. The band was leaving the pitch at Arms Park and *nothing* was going to interrupt the next ninety minutes of bliss. Except of course, the muzzle of Idwal's automatic as it gently carressed the back of his ear.

"If you want to hear the end of the match, boyo, then get your master key and lock up those three engaged, right, butty?" said Idwal in the sternest voice he could muster.

The little attendant replaced his peak cap to do as he was told.

"Right!" shouted Idwal with a slight tremor in his voice. "You are all hostages. No 'arm will come to you if you do as you're told."

Taking the key from the bewildered attendant, he ushered him back to the Wash and Brush Up.

"Don't miss the match on my account, boyo," he said as he locked him in. He turned to face the three occupants of the cubicles as they peered over the tops of their prisons doors whilst standing on the seats.

"Well, I can see that one of you is a froggie, but don't worry, I brought a transistor so you won't miss the match. Oh 'ell, I don't suppose you'll understand a word of it. Never mind, we'll manage to let you know the score, won't we, boys?"

"It don't worry me who wins," replied one obviously Irish brogue.

"And I am not worrying as well," said the third hostage in a sing-song Asian accent.

Above ground an anxious crowd of men peered down the steps to the Gents as Idwal spoke through a small loud hailer pressed to the keyhole. It was the unintentional pun that brought timid laughter from the hard-pressed listeners. "Sorry for the inconvenience, gents," he said. "But I have four hostages down here. If someone tells the police like, I'll state my terms to them, innit."

At that moment Sergeant Sidney Hawksworth of the Cardiff Anti-Terrorist Squad arrived on his bicycle. His steel-grey eyes slowly scanned the area as he removed his trouser clips before stealthily descending the steps. He spoke through the keyhole in an anti-terrorist manner.

"Sergeant Hawksworth here, son, of the Special Branch. Now keep a cool head and answer my questions, okay. Are you British or foreign?"

He put his ear to the keyhole for a reply only to jump back in pain as Idwal answered through his loud hailer.

"Neither. I'm Welsh."

"Could 'ave told me you had one of them things," said the sergeant, still rubbing his pierced eardrum. "Well, what organisation are you? The P.L.O.? The F.L.O.? The C.L.O.? or just the L.O.?"

He stood well back from the keyhole for the reply.

"None of them," said Idwal. "I represent the G.M.F.L.O."

"Who the 'ell are they?" said the sergeant. "That's a new crowd to me."

"The Gilfach Mawr Fish Liberation Organisation," replied Idwal.

"We got a right one here," whispered the sergeant up the steps to his constables. "Better stand by with a strait jacket."

"Aye," shouted Idwal. "I want safe conduct for me and fifteen fish to Libya."

"Libya?" queried the sergeant. "I'd 'a thought Llangorse Lake or Roath Park, but not Libya. It's all sand, no good for fish, 'sides he's a funny sort out there, he might not take to you, like. Not to mention the fish."

A giant roar suddenly vibrated across Cardiff, causing all heads to turn in the direction of Arms Park and for a moment the siege of the Hayes Public Convenience was completely ignored by all.

"Was that a Welsh try, sergeant?" shouted Idwal through the keyhole. "Sounded like one, the French sound different, don't they?"

"Aye," said the learned sergeant. "That's because they talk through their noses a lot. They cheer through their noses as well. Come to think of it, boyo, why don't you go back to Paris with the French supporters tonight. There's half a dozen of their planes at Cardiff Airport. Save the taxpayer 'ell of a packet if you and your fish would ship out with them instead of Libya, like."

"My mind's made up," replied Idwal nervously. "If you don't meet my demands by noon tomorrow, I'll blow this bog to blazes, innit."

"Right then," said the sergeant. "I can see a long night before us, but first things first: there'll be all 'ell let loose when that lot starts boozing later with nowhere to relieve themselves."

"More like a flood, I'd 'ave thought," said a constable.

"That's what I mean," retorted the sergeant. "Cycle over to the public works department, tell 'em to get a large portable loo here right away before mass hysteria breaks out."

Below ground Idwal prepared for the night.

"Sorry you got to sleep upright, boys," he said to the three men in the cubicles. "We'll have a nice supper first, though. Just tell me what you fancy and I'll order it off the sergeant. They never let you starve. I've seen it all on telly. Mind you, I 'ope they don't use the S.A.S., they can cut up rough, those boys."

The sergeant, however, failed to be impressed with the international menu that Idwal slipped under the door.

"Now look here, boyo," he said. "You might be an emotional, temperamental, highly dangerous terrorist, but I'm not chasing all over Cardiff for this lot, it's pie and chips for all of you, right?"

"Done," said the hungry Idwal. "I don't know why they're so fussy, mind you, but seeing as how you're going to the chippy, we'll all 'ave a carton of curry to go with it, like."

The fish now swam in the tranquil cistern tanks, for Idwal had long since turned off the water supply to stop the flushing. Standing on a chair borrowed from the Wash and Brush Up, he fondly sprinkled food to his charges.

"There you are, my beauties, soon be out of here, we will. No more of that blasted flushing every 'arf 'our. Must be on the verge of a breakdown, some of you looks quite depressed already, mun."

On the surface, the Hayes resembled an American movie scene as the blue lamps of police cars and ambulances rotated like disco lights, and noisy motor generators supplied power to the batteries of arc lamps that all converged on the steps to the Gents. John Batchelor gazed down in awe at the portable loo below as international merrymakers accepted the saga of Idwal and his fish in carnival spirit. As dawn illuminated the litter-strewn capital, a helicopter began to descend near John Batchelor.

"This is it then, Idwal," said the sergeant with emotionally misted eyes. "Get the fish ready."

Press cameras whirred as the attendant came up first, proudly wearing his peaked cap with the Parks and Baths Department badge, followed by the Asian gentleman, the French gentleman and the Irish gentleman, followed by Idwal wearing his black bag, a machine gun in one hand and a large plastic water-filled bag of fish in the other. The scene, which could have been highly emotional, was spoilt only by one massive discord of voices as the Cardiff Asian Society, the Cardiff Irish Society, the Cardiff French Society and the supporters of Idwal all sang their various anthems simultaneously.

The firemen boarded the helicopter followed by Sergeant Hawksworth and Idwal. As as the door closed, the rotors began to spin. The craft rose until Cardiff grew quite small and John Batchelor, now covered in traffic cones, was barely discernable. Idwal was too nervous to query the use of a helicopter instead of a plane and completely ignorant of the fact that it flew up and down the Bristol channel thirty-six times before hovering over Steepholm, the long whale-like island just a half a dozen miles from Cardiff.

"That's it, then," said Sergeant Hawksworth, six hours after take-off from John Batchelor and the Hayes loo. "Get the fish ready, boyo, we'll be down in five minutes."

"Don't look much like Libya to me," said Idwal. "I thought there'd be more sand like."

"Time of the year," said the fast-thinking sergeant. "Everythings growing well and covered it right now."

And the 'copter gently settled on the thick gorse blanket of Idwal's future home. You might spot him as you pass near by on the pleasure steamer, and if you land don't be surprised if he shakes your hand and says, "Pleased to meet you, Colonel . . ."

And as for the fish, well, they don't seem to have done too badly for themselves, despite their freshwater heritage. Ironically the Gilfach Mawr Sea Angling Society landed a pink fish near Steepholm. It baffled the experts, who could only reach the conclusion that it was a cross between a cod and a goldfish.

CHAPTER
TWELVE

"The Man with the Marigold Tie"

On a foggy November morning of 1936, "Pugh the Pill" was put to rest after providing a health service second to none to the inhabitants of Mid-Rhondda for more than three decades. Like all Welsh tradesmen, that was his nickname of course. The true title over his shop, inscribed in gold leaf on a black background, was "Emrys J. Pugh M.P.S." He had other nicknames, such as "Pugh the Prescription" and one that was mentioned only by the menfolk of the town, "Pugh the Preventative". But in those unpromiscuous thirties the subject of birth control had an obscene classification and the birth-stopping condom was ordered with an embarrassed whisper to the barber or chemist. No female ever provided the little rubber balloon. No female ever even conceded its existence. "It was part of man's anatomy," they naïvely convinced themselves.

And that was the problem for Widow Pugh. Emrys, you see, had had an excellent rapport with his condom clients. From his raised glass-fronted dispensary, he would survey the shoppers over the top of his half-spectacles as he prepared their prescriptions. A prospective condom purchaser was quickly recognised as the blushing male entered the shop with a flourish of built-up bravado. He would take a stance just inside the doorway and direct his appealing eye-language to the ever-vigilant Mr Pugh.

Mrs Pugh, if she was not serving another customer, would cast an acid glare at the lecherous sex maniac, and turn to polish the seemingly endless wall of small wooden drawers with glass knobs and Latin names behind her. Her very appearance, puritan to the core, was hardly compatible to such a phallic emblem as the condom. Her well-washed face with no trace of cosmetics. Her tightly bunned jet hair. Her long slender neck adorned with a black band and a cameo and her full length sombre dress was totally alien to a symbol of debauchery and fornication. Mr Pugh's mode of dress and appearance were equally conservative. A dapper man with fine dark hair, well-sodden in Brilliantine and with a centre parting so precise that it may have been arranged with a slide rule. His narrow Hitler moustache shone with a fine black-dyed lustre to contrast with the intense white of his perfect, symmetrical dentures.

But the little chemist was a shrewd entrepreneur and the handsome profit margin of the contraceptive lured him from his dispensary like a greyhound from the trap. The ritual never varied. The customer homed on that part of the counter where the little brass gas pipe rose like a phoenix to wax and seal the prescribed medicines of the doctor's choice. Not a word was said as a half a crown was produced, the exact cost of a packet of three. With a slight smile, Mr Pugh would turn to the drawer marked "Lict Tinc Ani", beautifully sign-written in rich gold paint, to procure the little envelope with all the subtle discretion of a retail diplomat. Not for nothing had his reputation earned him the title of "Pugh the Preventative", in stark contrast to his arch-rival, Davies the Barber who sold his rubber goods without the slightest hint of secrecy before an audience of waiting haircuts.

But now Mr Pugh and his discretion had gone, much to the delight of the hairdresser who smirked at the impossibility of the straight-laced Widow Pugh selling "Frenchies". Mrs Pugh was undaunted. The dispenser had always sold the disgusting things and the replacement for her husband would carry on the tradition. She had not taken into her assumptions, however, the growing trend of a feminine intrusion into the male-dominated world of the pharmacist, for the sole applicant was Esther Runcorn, a woman no less.

They confronted each other beneath the three huge glass flasks of coloured water that had stood like sentinels in the shop for as long as anyone could remember. Miss Runcorn's credentials were perfect, thought Mrs Pugh as she summed up the middle-aged spinster.

"But what about the . . . the things, the rubber goods?"

"Only with dark glasses," replied Miss Runcorn, as if expecting the subject to arise. "I'd sell them, yes, I'd sell them, but only when wearing dark glasses".

Mrs Pugh was elated. Her respectability could remain untarnished, her prestige as she played the organ at Ebenezer Chapel would remain invincible and guiltless.

But what about the traveller, the man from the British Rubber Company, the rubber goods salesman? she thought. She rushed into the storeroom for a stiff tipple of iron tonic wine to steady her nerves. Emrys had always seen to him, upstairs in the living room, of course, out of earshot of everyone. Her right hand toyed nervously with the cameo at the throat.

"He's due next week," she whispered to herself. "A nice man really, a proper gentleman, but the things he sells." She poured another eight fluid ounces of tonic into the tapered medicine measure. "Can't ask Miss Runcorn to see to him." A maiden lady upstairs alone, in her living room, with a rubber goods salesman. No, that would never do even if Miss Runcorn agreed, dark glasses or no dark glasses. She poured a third measure, and her mind became more rational as her whole body warmed with the intake of the tonic alcohol. "I'll see him," she said loudly as she asserted herself before the little wall mirror. "He's no different to the other travellers, it's just what he sells, the disgusting things."

A week later, in which time Miss Runcorn had provided yeoman service as the official dispenser of prescribed medicines and rubber goods, wearing dark glasses for the latter of course, the traveller in rubber goods arrived. Mrs Pugh's hand froze to a bottle of gripe water she was serving as she recognised his figure at the front of the shop. Her heart began to thump as she realised the pending trauma of her first encounter with him. A bit like Ronald Coleman the film star, she thought, with his dark pinstripe suit and his thin moustache, his red carnation, his crisp new handkerchief in his breast-pocket and his tie, yes of course the tie, dark maroon with little orange marigolds all over it.

That was the discreet symbol of his company, a silent announcement of his presence, a warning not to be approached by any female member of the staff who might be embarrassed. Mrs Pugh gave a weak smile as she completed her gripe water sale.

"Good morning, Mr Cartwright, will you come this way, please?" she said with a tremor. "And Miss Runcorn, will you take over the counter for awhile?"

The dispenser, without a word but with features portraying abject disgust, followed their movements as the couple began the ascent to the living room. Well, from that day Mrs Pugh became a new woman. She confided in Miss Runcorn that she felt stronger after her confrontation with Basil Cartwright.

"I feel that I have struck a note for womanhood," she said. "A move towards equality, in the chemist shops at least."

Her new-found confidence also made its mark on the shop by way of several improvements and she even accepted Mr Cartwright's offer of a very subtle and discreet sign for his products. With the increased trade she decided to engage an assistant.

"A school leaver," she told Mr Proctor at the Labour Exchange. "'She,' will have to be a girl," she insisted with a one-sided attitude to her version of equality. "There's lots of lines in a chemist shop that only a woman is capable of handling, you know."

The successful applicant was Gwenny James, a tall slender awkward girl with an outgoing personality. Mrs Pugh deemed her to have an intellectual appearance befitting a chemist, with her smooth jet black hair cut like a German helmet, and her small wire-rimmed spectacles resting on a powderless nose. Her training was thorough and Mrs Pugh supervised her every move like a mother hen over a chick. From day one she constantly received instructions regarding the man with the marigold tie.

"You see, Gwenny," Mrs Pugh repeated. "He sells things that you're too young to know about, so don't forget, I always see to him, and if I'm upstairs in the living room, just you run up and tell me, do you understand?"

"Yes, Mrs Pugh," replied Gwenny. "Miss Runcorn warned me about him as well. She calls him the preventative man. What does he prevent, Mrs Pugh?"

"Should have prevented you," thought Mrs Pugh as she stormed into the rear storeroom.

Three weeks later, Mrs Pugh was afflicted with one of her rare migraine attacks. So intense was the pain that she remained confined to her living room with its rich velvet curtains drawn to obliterate all natural light. And in the shop beneath, Miss Runcorn dispensed her medicines with spasmodic pauses to don her sunglasses and serve her rubber goods clientele, while Gwenny tried to fathom what the little envelopes prevented.

Suddenly as she turned from the till to present the change for a bottle of backache and kidney pills, her body became as stiff as a pitprop. There he was, and no Mrs Pugh to see to him. Her eyes became transfixed on his tie with a mixed expression of amazement and fear as he smiled back at her, and Miss Runcorn ignored him from the privacy of her glass-fronted dispensary.

"I'll . . . I'll tell Mrs Pugh you're here," said Gwenny, backing away to the foot of the staircase. In a breathless speech she announced the arrival of the great man through a quarter-open door of the darkened living room.

"Tell him to come up, Gwenny," replied the sick woman with a feeble voice.

"She'll see you upstairs in the living room, sir," said Gwenny with a flourish of her arm towards the stairway. "The room's dark, mind you, she's got one of her headaches."

He knocked on the slightly open door.

"Come in," said Mrs Pugh in a soft sensuous tone. "I'm over here on the sofa, follow my voice."

The man's eyes became accustomed to the low light of the room as he gingerly approached her silhouette. She took his hand and pulled him towards her.

"Basil, my lover, how I've missed you, come closer; let me feel the warmth of your lips." But the man resisted as she tried to embrace him.

"I'm not Basil, Mrs Pugh," he stammered in muffled tones from her bosom. "I'm Emlyn Evans the new minister of Ebenezer. Come to introduce myself, I have."

CHAPTER
THIRTEEN

The Wild West

Of all the humorous nicknames within the large Evans clan of Gilfach Mawr, perhaps "Eighteen Months Evans" was the strangest. Having lost a half of his right ear to a hungry prop forward in a vicious rugby scrummage, he was left with a ear and a half, hence "Eighteen Months."

His disfigurement caused little problem until he joined "The Gilfach Mawr Wild West Society" as a bank robber and his black Stetson hat blatantly refused to sit squarely on his head. The trouble was that it tilted to the right in a rakish angle where it rested on the remaining lower half of his ear.

"You can't rob a bloody bank with yer hat like that," said Tex Lewis, the Chairman of the society. "You got to look a mean bugger with yer hat firmly on yer head, not half-cocked like that. They'll take you for a poofter, they will."

"But we're only playing," argued Eighteen Months.

"I know that," replied Tex. "But we got to be factual like. What's the sense in having a bloody society if we ain't factual, init?"

"But I looks bloody mean when I put my neck scarf over my face, don't I?" replied Evans.

"No. You still looks a poofter 'an if you don't do something with that ear 'ole of yours, I'm afraid you're out of the society."

Poor Eighteen Months. He tried everything to disguise his half ear. He tried making up the top part with plasticine, but it fell off just as he began to rob his first fictitious bank in the mirror. He tried moulding the ear with pottery clay but his prowess as a sculptor left a lot to be desired, and when he fitted the bizarre oversize ear over his half ear, he took on the appearance of the Elepbant Man.

"It's no good," said the Chairman at the next meeting of the society. "You'll never make a desperado with that 'arf a lughole of yours. You'll 'ave to do something else, like."

"But who's to know I didn't get it shot off in a gun fight with the Marshal?" pleaded Eighteen Months. "You're always on about being factual. What's more factual than that?"

Tex shook his head. "Did you ever see any of the Hollywood desperados with 'arf a lug 'ole and a lopsided hat like Noël Coward wears?"

"But this is bloody Gilfach Mawr, not Hollywood," answered Evans.

"Aye. That's where you're wrong, butty. Hollywood can be seen even in the Gilfach flea pit cinema, can't it, boys?" said the Chairman triumphantly.

With the roar of approval from the members, Eighteen Months realised his days as a desperado were over.

"I'm sorry," said the Chairman. "But we've got a following of astute western fans an' they'll pick on your 'arf ear in a flash, they will."

"But what if he wears a smaller hat?" said a voice from the back. He was Seedy Evans who played the part of the chief cashier in the Bank of Dodge City.

"An 'ave it stuck on 'is head like Laurel and Hardy do?" replied the Chairman with an acid glare at the little man wearing a green sunshield over his eyes.

"I tell you what we can do," began Doc Haliday Jenkins, the club secretary.

"What's that, then?" asked the Chairman.

"Well, Dai Santos who takes the money for the gold mine visits wants to be an Indian chief, an he'd make a good un too. He's half Spanish, see. If we make him into an Indian, then Eighteen Months could 'ave his job, see like?"

"But there's no action in that job," pleaded Evans. "I want action, see. That's why I joined the society in the first place."

"There's plenty of bloody action in that ole mine," replied the secretary. "Chasing all the young vandals out of there."

The gold mine was an abandoned drift coal mine in the Cwm Valley, made authentic with the use of gold paint. Three-foot wide coal seams shone with the magic lustre of Eldorado and drams full of gold-painted coal nuggets represented a king's ransom in value.

"All you gotta do is paint over the previous day's graffiti on the gold seams before you start taking the money at the entrance, like," said the chairman as he introduced Eighteen Months to his new job the following weekend.

"But what about the action?" asked Evans.

"Once a month," replied the chairman. "It's a special feature that we've planned. The desperados will raid the mine once a month an' you've got to try and defend it. They'll beat you up a bit. Can't help it, see, but there's your action, init."

Evans accepted his new position under protest. Despite his Old West form of dress as a mine-worker, he was easily recognized by the inhabitants of Gilfach Mawr when they bought their tickets for the mine. It was while he repainted the gold seams in the mine one day that good fortune struck him literally. A large lump of what he thought to be painted coal fell from the top of the seam to land painfully on his shoulder.

"That's funny," he murmured to himself, "It's painted all over. How the hell can that be?" He looked up at the hole from where the lump had fallen. "That's as black as the halls of hell. So how come this piece is painted all over, like?" he continued.

He took it back to his ticket office, where he tried to crack it with a hammer but the stubborn lump refused to break. The following morning he took it to the bank. The cashier's face had a puzzled expression when he placed it on the counter. "I was wondering if you can tell me if that's gold or not, like. If it is, I'll bank it, like."

"I'm afraid you will have to take it to a metallurgist," replied the cashier.

"Is there one in Gilfach?" asked Evans.

"No," replied the cashier. "You'll have to go down Cardiff to find one."

Evans left the bank with a feeling of elation. This really was the authentic Wild West that the Chairman of the Society kept on about. Now he was a gold prospector.

His find proved to be a record-breaking nugget of Welsh gold. To stop any claims on it, Evans had stated that it was his late grandfather's who always thought it to be a big lump of brass. It made him quite rich and he announced that his new-found wealth was the result of a football pools win. But his desire to be a desperado in the society haunted him. He tried to bribe his way into the part but while every member of the community was eager to accept his offer, they feared exposure, and the result was a resolute refusal to receive his offer of a substantial donation to the funds.

"I got to rob a bloody bank," he repeatedly said to himself as he sat in his ticket office each weekend. "I got to prove to them that I can do it even with a 'ear and a half an' a lopsided hat, like."

That evening he donned his desperado clothes and spun his revolvers before his wardrobe mirror, but as he began to plan the real thing his bravado started to diminish. "Could be a bit risky," he said to the mirror. "I'll give it all back to them, but still it could be dodgy, like."

He thought of Davies the Sweet Shop and Jones the Grocer and even Rees the Butcher, but that would not be authentic, running from their shops with guns blazing. No. It had to be a bank. Suddenly it came to him. The Valley Building Society. A one-man band, or woman in this case: Old Miss Hopgood. Aye. Only her ran the old show, not that many people ever used the place, but it is a bank, he assured himself.

The following day he trembled with excitement as he dressed in his desperado clothes and his record player produced a tune from a spaghetti western. Precisely at noon, for that seemed to be the most authentic time, he kicked open the door of the Valley Building Society. His spurs jingled as he walked to the counter where a bespectacled old lady looked up at him without the slightest indication of surprise.

"Yes?" she said. "Can I help you?"

"It's a robbery!" said Evans brandishing his two replica guns. "Just hand me your cash and you will not be harmed."

"It's Eighteen Month Evans, isn't it?" said Miss Hopgood. "You don't look much of a building society robber with your hat one-sided. Not like they look in the films anyway. That's for sure."

"You're not s'posed to be a Building Society," pleaded Evans. "You're s'posed to be the Dodge City Bank. I'm practising see."

At that moment the eighteen-stone police constable Parry, who thought it strange for an armed cowboy to enter the Building Society, became suspicious and he decided to investigate and brought Evans down with a rugby tackle. The trouble was that P.C. Parry was prone to ear biting and he severed the top of Evan's left ear.

Evans received three years for attempted robbery but it's an ill wind that blows some good and he now wears his hat quite squarely on his head and is fully accepted as a desperado in the Wild West Society. His nickname has changed however. He is now known as "TWELVE MONTHS EVANS."

CHAPTER
FOURTEEN

The Ferret

Crevice Hughes, the landlord of the Colliers Arms took his false teeth from their jar of water beneath the bar counter, in preparation for opening time. He bothered little about his appearance for the morning trade, but he felt that the evening trade required more dignity to his appearance. Soon his totally toothless, gums that caused the concave in his facial features and the obvious nickname of Crevice, were dressed overall in a complete set of NHS dentures. He scattered fresh sawdust over the pine floor in readiness for the few six o'clock regulars who were waiting outside in shaking anticipation of their alcoholic replenishment.

"I got to change the image of this place," said Crevice to himself. "The days of the spit and sawdust are gone, like. I got to 'ave a posh lounge with carpet like them Cardiff pubs, I have."

He opened the door to admit Delirium Davies, the drunkard of Gilfach Mawr. For thirty years he had been first over the threshold to consume the magic elixir that had caused his shake in the first place. Crevice looked at him with contempt as he placed his first pint on the counter before him.

"I been thinking of telling the Guinness Book of Records about you, Dell."

Davies raised his froth-covered lips from his drink like a chicken at a water trough. It was too early in the evening to hold the glass in his vibrating hands.

"Why's that, Crevice?" asked Dell, "I haven't drunk that much, 'ave I?"

"That's debatable," answered Crevice. "I'll bet you're up there with the champions, but I was thinking more of your uninterrupted attendance for thirty years."

The second habitual regular arrived in the form of Snaky Evans, the poacher. His mud-sodden boots left a trail of sawdust footprints as he approached the bar. He felt in the lining of his ex-bus driver's overcoat to produce a pair of dead rabbits, which caused a rapid movement beneath his buttoned collar-less shirt.

"Quiet, girl!" he shouted to the ferret inside who was aroused by the movement of her dead quarry. "Do you want these for a quid, Crevice?" he asked the landlord.

"I s'ppose so," answered Crevice. "But if I eat many more I'll be getting to look like Bugs Bunny myself."

The bar began to fill with its usual complement of homeward-bound workers calling for their aperitifs. While some, like Delirium Davies and Snaky Evans, thought they were home and settled down for the evening. Crevice looked through the small window at the rear of the bar to a fine split-level bungalow in the centre of the sloping five acre field. "Nearly ready?" he shouted over his shoulder to one of the builders at the bar.

"Aye," answered Jack the Brick. "He'll be moving in a week or two. Not a bad job is it, like? Bought the field an' all, he ave."

Crevice came to the counter and after looking both ways in a manner of someone with a great secret to impart, he spoke to the builder. "I been thinking of some alterations myself, Jack. I been thinking about converting the old billiard room into a lounge bar like. No-one uses it these days since the moths ate the cloth. It's down to the slate."

Jack pushed his empty glass toward him for a refill.

"Good idea, Crevice. You need somewhere a bit posher than this bar to take the missus to, don't you? Even the Karl Marx Club 'ave got a bit of carpet in one room, but they still don't allow women, mind you, 'cept on bingo night, like."

Crevice adopted his manner of secrecy again. "Do you fancy having a go at it, Jack?" he asked. "At the right price, mind you."

Jack looked behind the bar to the beer store beyond.

"Will your beer pipes be coming from there, Crevice?" he asked.

"Aye," replied the landlord. "Underground, like, across this bar, then a sharp turn into the hall, then into the billiard room bar when it's built, like."

Jack's cement-grained hands rolled a cigarette as he dwelt on the plan. "I'd have to lay a line of drain pipes under the floor and you could feed your plastic beer pipes through them, like."

It was midnight, and much haggling had taken place, before a price was agreed. "We'll do the lounge bar first," said Jack. "Then we'll tackle the pipeline. We've to do that at night, cause we got to dig the floor of this bar, an' you can't do that with customers in here, can you?"

"I don't suppose half of 'em would notice once they've had few pints, but we'll stick to the night plan for that job," answered Crevice.

A month later Crevice stood with pride on the newly laid carpet of his lounge. "Like another world after the old spit and sawdust, init?" he said to Jack the Brick, who stood beside him.

"Aye" replied Jack. "We'll start tonight on the pipeline for the beer an' you'll soon be ready for your grand opening. Any idea who'll do that for you?"

"I was thinking of the Town Clerk," replied Crevice. "Considering that he's my neighbour now."

The Colliers Arms vibrated that night as pneumatic drills cut into the concrete floor of the pub to make a trench for the pottery drain pipes that would house eighty feet of plastic beer pipe from the beer store to the lounge. By dawn they were laid and covered with fresh concrete, but as Jack the Brick walked wearily home to his house in Pant Street, he suddenly stopped and slapped his forehead with his right band.

"Bugger it," he said aloud. "We haven't fed the beer pipe through as we laid it."

That evening he confronted Crevice with the daunting news. They tried pushing the pliable plastic through the pipeline but it stubbornly stopped when at the first joint just four feet along.

116

"I reckon I can solve that problem," said a voice from the bar-counter amongst the audience watching the two men struggle in the surface cellar just four steps below. It was Snaky Evans, the poacher. "Blodwyn will do the job for you."

"Bugger off, Snaky," replied an exasperated Crevice as he straightened upright from his futile task. "We got problems enough without your wisecracks. Who the hell is Blodwyn, in any case?"

"She's here, in my shirt," answered Snaky. "Blodwyn's my ferret, init like."

Crevice dismissed the poacher with a push of his hand. "I told you that strong beer would get you in the end, boyo. If we can't shove the bloody pipe along, how the hell d'you think that rat of yours is going to do it? You bin watching too many Mickey Mouse cartoons, I reckon."

Snaky ignored his sneers. "I'll need a ball of strong twine and about eighty foot of good rope."

The landlord and the builder looked at each other before bursting into uncontrollable laughter.

"Where do Blodwyn come into this, then?" asked Crevice as he wiped the tears from his eyes with a bent index finger. Snaky remained straight-faced, immune to the taunts of his tormentor.

"Get me the twine for starters, like, an' I'll show you, innit."

Jack the Builder tapped Crevice on his shoulder. "Let's give it a try, Crev. You never know with these dopey buggers, they sometimes get a streak of genius in 'em."

Crevice ambled off to his junk room. "We must be as daft as he is," he shouted over his shoulder, and after some considerable rummaging he returned with a fully loaded sea fishing reel.

"Is this any good?" he asked the poacher.

"Aye," said Snaky. "That's good strong stuff is that. Now I'll tie one end around Blodwyn's neck." He reached in to where Blodwin, sensing she was about to go on a hunting mission, was excitedly moving about inside his shirt. Crevice and Jack looked dumbbounded as he offered them the tethered ferret. "Now I'll go into the lounge and call her through the drain pipe, then you let her go from this end, see. While one of you plays out the line like, innit."

The two men looked at each other in continued amazement, one holding the fishing reel and one gingerly holding Blodwyn as her owner proceeded to the lounge.

"Right then," came the tubular command as he spoke through the pipe line. "Come on, Blod my beauty, come on girl, come to Snaky. I got a bit of rabbit for you, my lovely."

At the sound of her master's voice, Blodwyn sprang from the hands of a bewildered Crevice, while Jack the Brick let the line pay out from the fishing reel. The bar-counter was completely taken up with an excited audience who were totally ignorant of the content of the exercise.

"It's ferret training. That's what it is!" said Delirium Davies as Snaky appeared in the bar with his still tethered Blodwyn, both with a look of triumph in their eyes.

"The next stage is to tie a good rope to the fishing line your end, Crevice," he shouted over the crowd.

"Ah, I've got what he's up to," said Crevice to Jack excitedly. "We'll pull the rope through with the fishing line, then we'll tie the rope to the beer pipe, an' Bob's yer Uncle. We've done it, like."

Crevice discovered some rope, a coil of strong marine anchor rope that he had taken in exchange for two pints one evening. Snarky put Blodwyn back in his shirt, happily chewing her reward of raw rabbit meat, and pulled the rope through to the lounge with just a little resistance as it stuck at the numerous joints along the pipe line.

"Now for the beer pipe," he shouted along the tube, and with bated breath the audience watched the shining new plastic pipe enter its tunnel as it snaked from the coil. Suddenly it stopped.

"Are we through?" shouted Crevice through the tube.

"No!" came the answer from Snaky. "I reckon we're stuck on the bend in the hall. We need a few more hands this end to move it, like."

A body of volunteers rushed to Snaky's aid, eager to earn a free pint from Crevice for services rendered. They pulled with all the zest of a Tug O' War team, but the fickle beer pipe wouldn't budge.

"I tell you what" said Jack the Brick. "I'll take my van into the Town Clerk's field and try pulling it with that, like."

"You'll snap it, won't you?" said one pessimistic customer.

"No bloody fear" replied Crevice. "It'll stretch a bit, but it won't break. It's stronger than rope, is that pipe."

They fed the rope through the lounge window before fastening it to the van.

"Pull away, boys," said Snaky, who had now adopted the attitude of foreman of the procedure. Blue smoke belched from the exhaust of Jack's van as the rope became taut and its wheels began to skid, but the stubborn beer pipe wouldn't yield an inch. Suddenly the wheels ceased spinning as the engine raged even faster.

"That's it!" shouted Jack as he switched off. "I've burnt my bloody clutch out. You lot had better shove me back on to the street. Don't want that little bugger to know I been in his field. He'll prosecute at the drop of a hat, he will."

The following evening Crevice opened his front door as usual to Delirium Davies and Snaky Evans. "I ought to ban you, Snaky," he said. "You and that bloody ferret idea of yours."

"Half a mo, half a mo, Crevice," replied Snaky. "I been rabbiting up by the open cast coal site an' I was telling Digger Lewis about your problem. Well, he drives one of them bloody great dumper trucks. It'll go anywhere, like, an' he said he'll pull your pipe through for fifty quid."

"Fifty quid!" exploded Crevice without his teeth that he had forgotten to fit in his depression. "This bloody lounge is gonna cost more than the London Dorchester before it's finished."

"Calm down an' put your teeth in, Crevice," replied Snaky. "You're bloody drowning me, you are."

"Try him for forty quid," said Crevice, with a clearer diction once his dentures were fitted. "But he'll 'ave to do it when the Town Clerk is in work. He won't like it to find that bloody great thing in his field by his posh new bungalow."

"He'll do it in his grub time."

"That's okay, then," replied Crevice. "He's at the Town Hall all day."

"Forty quid, mind you. And a couple of free pints for me, like, innit," said Snaky.

The following day the Colliers shook as if suffering from an earthquake and the bar went dark to announce the arrival of the fifty tonne dumper truck.

"You strikes an 'ard bargain, you does," said Digger Lewis. "This machine costs a small fortune."

"Not to you it don't," said Crevice. "Now let's get on with it. I'll see you in the field."

Crevice was dwarfed by the giant machine as he tied the rope to its towing hook before a large assembled audience who were receiving a running commentary from Snaky Evans.

"Take it steady now!" shouted Crevice to the driver. "That thing could pull the pub down."

Once again the rope went taut as the dumper's exhaust barked out and its monstrous wheels gripped the field, but still the cursed beer pipe refused to relinquish its grip. The towing rope began to squeal like a frightened rabbit as Digger inched forward, but it was only the mocking beer pipe stretching itself before the enthralled faces watching the drama. Suddenly, with the twang of a tight bow string, the reluctant beer pipe decided to capitulate and the totally unprepared dumper truck shot forward down the inclined field towards the Town Clerk's bungalow.

"Her brakes never was much cop," shouted Digger Lewis as he tried to stop the rampaging machine as it surged on with a death wish towards the doomed bungalow. A great cheer went up from the crowd as the residence was completely demolished.

Crevice was declared bankrupt after the affair and a large brewery bought the Colliers Arms. They turned it into a theme pub to commemorate the accident. The spit and sawdust bar was converted into a posh lounge and the billiard room, the cause of all the trouble, began to flourish as a restaurant. Crevice obtained a job as cellarman in the new pub, under its manager Mr Snaky Evans, who had convinced the brewery that he and Blodwyn were the instigators of the drama and therefore part of the theme of the pub.

Oh! by the way. The brewery also changed the name of the pub to "THE PIPE AND FERRET."

CHAPTER
FIFTEEN

"Nipper"

The two boys leaned against the fury of an autumn gale, shielding their eyes from the salt spindrift of the breakers coming with the evening flood tide. They looked down from the cliff top of Friars Point to the stricken vessel below, a French schooner who had foundered at the mercy of the dawn tide. Now it was returning with a death wish to complete its destruction.

Nipper, at ten the younger of the two, looked up at Roy, his brother, with traditional obedience. Like the other scavengers of the day they had come unashamedly for their share of the doomed ship's onion cargo. It was the frugal thirties when the spoils of a shipwreck could be a heaven-sent gift to desperate people. Behind them, an old discarded baby pram lay forlornly on its side, the pair of topmost wheels spinning slowly by wind power.

Roy hooked his thumbs behind his trouser braces to mimic his father. He cupped his bottom lip to blow the drizzle from his face. His sodden short black hair clung to his head like a skull cap as he impressed his brother with his senior status.

"We'll go down, Nipper," he said with a forceful tone of authority. The roar of the sea intensified as they reached its level, and Nipper looked in awe at the bowsprit above. His gaze travelled to the figurehead, a woman with golden laurels on her head. "Like the picture in school," he thought. "A Greek goddess." His eyes became fixed on hers, staring ahead in a mixture of terror and sadness. Nipper joined the sorrow of the beautiful lady. He thought of her sailing the seven seas, guiding her graceful ship to every corner of the world, and he sighed.

"Come on, Nipper," shouted his brother. "The tide's reached her stern."

They clambered up a rope ladder left by the previous salvagers, and Nipper suffered a feeling of guilt, a feeling that he was prying into the very soul of the beautiful lady at the bow. They peered into the hold as their nostrils took in the overpowering odour of the onion cargo. Roy pointed to a knotted rope hanging from the hatch combing.

"Down you go, Nipper, fill the basket an' I'll haul it up." The boy became insulated from the gale as he lowered himself down the rope, knot by knot, into an eerie silence.

Two hours later the exhausted boys pushed their overloaded pram though the front doorway of their terraced home. Their mother welcomed them with a hug and called to her husband in the parlour.

"You want to see them, Will, like a pair of drowned rats they are. Now strip off and hang your clothes on the horse, they'll be dry by the morning. My goodness, I've never seen so many onions."

Their father entered the room as they sat facing each other naked, taking in the warmth from the bright red fire of the blackleaded grate. He was a tall man with the hunched shoulders of an asthmatic. He felt shrouded with guilt that his sons should have been salvagers, but the thirties had injured the pride of many men who could not provide for their families. He greeted the boys with a broad smile.

"Well, lads, one thing's for sure we'll have plenty of onions for the stuffing this Christmas, but Lord knows what we're going to stuff. "

His words set Nipper thinking of the great day just a few weeks away. "Money makes Christmas worthwhile," he'd heard his father say, but money always seemed to be scarce in his house. He subconsciously stared at his father's heaving chest. He couldn't blame him really, too ill to work even when it was available. He recalled his Christmases of the past, the excitement of going to bed the evening before, the endurance of a near sleepless night, the revelation of the morning, the same as the year before and the year before that: one of his socks with an orange filling a hole in the heel, some nuts, an apple and a sugar mouse, a large parcel of newspaper that took hours to unravel for the threepenny piece at its core and, finally, the present, a Woolworth's sixpenny toy. He felt a pang of remorse for being so ungrateful, but why were they so poor?

Some of his friends had fathers with regular jobs and they has wonderful Christmas presents, and a turkey dinner, with crackers. No, his father was right, you

125

needed money to enjoy a good Christmas. His father interrupted his depressed train of thought.

"What was it like down the hold, Nipper? Roy said you had the jitters."

"A bit spooky really," said the boy. "I felt I was in a whale's belly like Jonah."

"You might have found a piece of ambergris amongst all those onions if it had been a whale," replied his father jokingly. His disability gave him much time to read and the free library was his cornucopia of knowledge.

"What's ambergris then?" asked Nipper.

His father put his atomiser to his nose, squeezing the rubber bulb once into each nostril. "It's a type of resin so I've read," he began. "Comes from sperm whales, they excrete it."

They were interrupted by his wife as she handed her sons a great coat each, one a bus driver's, the other a railwayman's, her spoils from a jumble sale.

"Now get these on, boys, an' come and have some stew. I've made fresh dumplings. And don't forget to put the coats back on your beds."

Nipper was eager with another question for his father. "What does excrete mean, Dad?" His mother promptly delayed her spouse's reply for she was a staunch member of the Band of Hope and even a word to describe a natural bodily function bordered on blasphemy.

"I hope you're not talking too old for them, Will," she said with an air of caution. "They're still only boys, remember."

Nipper pressed for his reply.

"Come on, Dad, what does it mean?" he asked, looking mischievously at his elder brother.

"Well, it means passing it, like going to the lavatory," the boys giggled as he continued. "It's very expensive, you know, they make ladies' scent out of it."

"Scent?" said Roy in surprise. "Scent out of something they've passed?"

"I wish I could find a lump of it," continued their father. "Lord knows how much it's worth."

"How would I know it on the beach, Dad?" asked Nipper. "What does it look like?"

"Not much chance of picking it up on our shore, son," his father replied. "No whales in this area, that's for certain," he winked one eye at Roy. "But keep your eyes skinned when you're down the beach, son, you never know. It's a greyish, blackish, soft blob of stuff, rounded by the sea no doubt, and there's not much smell to it according to the encyclopaedia."

Sunday arrived only too soon for Nipper. He added some variety to his enforced religious education by attending three churches. The Band of Hope, to satisfy his mother, the Methodist and the Baptist. There was no particular preference for any of them, except that their annual treats never occurred at the same time, and by obtaining a minimum of fifteen attendance stars at each school he enjoyed three outings a year.

His place of worship this Sunday was the Wesleyan Methodist, a posh church with an organ, and the first to get there pumped it for threepence. His mother vetted his appearance before he left. He wore his best tweed three-piece suit, the waistcoat pockets sporting a brass albert minus the watch. His black boots shone from their weekly polish to emphasise his grey woollen socks. She spat on her hand to pat down a stubborn tuft of hair on the crown of his head.

"There," she said, offering him a penny from a biscuit tin on the mantelpiece. "That's for collection, and don't you dare spend any of it on sweets."

She dispatched him with a kiss and a maternal smile as he left for the large grey church at the top of the hill. Miss Hawkesworthy the Sunday School teacher greeted him with an acid smile as they arrived together, and he claimed his right to pump the organ. She peered down at him over the top of her spectacles, a tall thin woman with tightly bunned black hair.

"I'm never sure," she began, as Nipper was joined by three more breathless boys, "whether you lads come for the love of Jesus or the revenue from the organ."

Nipper triumphantly took up his position by the long wooden handle of the instrument and the lesson began when a further two dozen children arrived. He listened intently as Miss Hawksworthy continued with her lesson, until finally she announced it was time to pray. "Put you hands together," she told her flock. "And talk to Jesus. First you ask him to forgive you for all your sins, and you pray for his help through life."

Nipper knelt on the pinewood floor of the church hall, his hands symmetrically arranged with care, fingers to fingers, thumbs to thumbs. He closed his eyes, and his lips moved with barely a whisper of his words.

He rushed through the forgiveness part of his offering to concentrate on the details requiring help.

"I want help to give help," he murmured. "I want to help my father, my mother and my brother, because they're so poor. I . . . I . . ." he thought of all the godly ways in which a sum of money could mysteriously arrive, but his mental search was futile. Then he remembered the ambergris. He recalled his father's words. "Not much chance of it washing up on our beach," he'd said. But Miss Hawkesworthy also said many times that "Jesus works in wondrous ways". He closed his eyes tighter, and pressed his hands harder.

"Please, Jesus," he whispered solemnly. "Please help me find a lump of ambergris."

Some weeks later he returned to the beach, joining the hordes of local children in the search for all that would burn on their Guy Fawkes bonfire. They trudged through the seaweed on the high water mark to reap their annual harvest of flotsam with an urgent sense of pyromania. Nipper returned for his second load, pulling his "bogie", a contraption of a plank and four perambulator wheels. He headed for the Bull Point, a quarter of a mile to the west of the bay, and soon he was alone, save for the company of a pair of gulls, who swooped in expectation of any morsel he might reveal as he kicked at the weed for concealed timber. Suddenly his lithe body became as stiff as the wood he was seeking. Ambergris! He knew it! He stared intently at the shining dark grey sphere nestling in the weed.

"Miss Hawkesworthy was right," he mumbled in wide-eyed amazement. "The Lord Jesus works in wondrous ways." His head turned up towards the dull November sky. "You must of heard me then, bloody hell, you heard me," he shouted.

The following evening saw him outside Llewellyn the chemist after school. Thankfully the shop was quiet, with only an old lady buying a tin of liver salts from Miss Hughes the assistant, while Mr Llewellyn made up a concoction behind his glass panelled dispensary. Nipper began to feel uneasy at the sight of him. He looked more like a headmaster than a chemist, a tall, thin man with jet black hair and a moustache liberally soaked in pomade. His long slender neck with a prominent adam's apple appeared lost in his starched white collar. He looked at Nipper over the top of his half spectacles with a weak smile. He was a sidesman at the Methodist and sometimes took the Sunday School when Miss Hawesworthy was unavailable. Nipper held up the sack-covered ball to him, and with a puzzled expression he came to the counter.

"It's about this," said Nipper in a loud whisper. "It's to do with scent, ladies' scent, an' I thought you might be able to help me."

Mr Llewellyn lightly scratched his immaculate hair with his second finger as two more customers arrived.

"In the dispensary, laddie," he said with an expression of discomfort. They faced each other against a countless array of dark brown jars with latin names in gold-leaf, crowned on the top shelf by the sign of the pharmacist, three huge glass flasks of coloured water.

"It's about the power of prayer an' this ball of ambergris, Mr Llewellyn," stammered Nipper. "Miss Hawksworthy told us how Jesus works in wondrous ways an' she was right. I prayed for a lump of ambergris an' I found it down the beach."

"Ambergris?" queried the chemist, while staring hard at the sphere. "How do you know it's ambergris?"

"I'm positive," replied Nipper. "Jesus sent it, I know he did. I stuck to the rules, you see, I didn't pray for myself, I asked him for a piece of ambergris so as I could help my family have a decent Christmas for a change." His large brown eyes pleaded with Mr Llewellyn. "D'you want to buy it, sir?"

The chemist struggled for a suitable answer. "We don't really know if it is ambergris, my lad, and if it is, I don't make perfume, so it would be of no use to me."

Nipper's eyes remained focused on his.

"But you could sell it to the people who make scent, couldn't you, Mr Llewellyn?"

The chemist gave a shrug, and a sigh of defeat. "Very well, then, I'll have it analysed, but don't you bank on being rich until I find out what it is, d'you hear?"

However, the chemist's warning was ignored as Nipper stood on the sawdust floor of the butcher's shop two doors away.

"Could I order a Christmas turkey, please?" he asked.

The butcher paused in his wrapping of a purchase. "That's a bit of a tall order for your family, my boy," he replied with a smile and a wink of his eye. "Better wait an' see what your mother says about that."

131

"No, no, she mustn't know," cried Nipper, with indignation. "It's to be a surprise from me, see. I've got some money coming, an' I'm going to give 'em a good Christmas. Just you put my name down for a turkey, Mr Sharpe, I'll pay for it, don't you worry."

The butcher took his pencil from his ear and wrote on a sheet of greaseproof paper. "All right, my lad, I'll see to that, now off you go." And he crumpled it in his hand as the boy danced from the shop.

Barely a shop in the high street was missed, his reception varied from cold cynicism to jocular acceptance of his orders, but Nipper was totally convinced that Jesus in his wondrous way was guiding him toward the best Christmas of his life.

The following day it was his turn to attend the Methodist, and he had made a bold decision. For three-quarters of an hour he sat on the steps of the Sunday School awaiting the arrival of Miss Hawkesworthy. She eyed him with her usual suspicion as she put the key in the door.

"Don't look so concerned, boy, you're first, you can pump the organ and earn your threepence."

"I don't want it, Miss," replied Nipper quickly. "I'll do it for nothing."

The teacher stared hard at him with one hand on her waist.

"For nothing? My goodness, I find this hard to believe."

"I've changed, Miss," explained Nipper. "Ever since you told us about the power of prayers. I tried it an' it works, Miss. I prayed to help others an' it works, I'm going to give my family their best Christmas ever."

Miss Hawkesworthy patted his shoulder with a rare display of affection.

And so came Christmas Week.

"Good news," said Mr Llewellyn, in his dispensary. Nipper's eyes became larger as the chemist unfolded his story. "It was valuable, and I've sold it for you. I've used the money to pay for all the goods that you ordered."

Nipper embraced his waist as tears flowed down his cheeks.

"You have a busy time before you now," continued Mr Llewellyn. "Just you pop along to all the shops. They'll be expecting you."

The most difficult part of Nipper's venture was to convince his parents of his integrity when he displayed the goods in the front parlour of their house.

"I thought there was something fishy going on," said his mother with her arms akimbo. "He hasn't been himself for weeks, Will."

"But I haven't pinched it, Mam," answered Nipper defiantly. "I bought it with ambergris."

His mother looked toward her husband. "You put that into his head, Will, what does he mean?" He beckoned his wife to leave the room with him, to the passage, where he spoke in a whisper.

"I've known about this for some weeks now, Mr Llewellyn the Chemist told me. Nipper's gone all religious. He believes Jesus has led him to a piece of ambergris and he wanted to sell it to provide us with a good Christmas."

She grasped her husband's hand. "Oh, God bless him, Will, that's why he's been so strange; and he was just thinking of us all the time."

He put his hand to her lips. "Mr Llewellyn said we should co-operate with him, not to daunt his faith, like," he nodded towards the parlour. "Looks like he did find ambergris, going by that lot in there, and Mr Llewellyn sold it for him."

His wife was speechless as tears streamed down her face to converge at her chin and drip to her bosom. Together they entered the parlour to thank their son, and the three embraced each other in joyful tears.

* * *

Eighteen years later, the Reverend David Brooke, alias Nipper, was inducted into the very church of his childhood reformation. During a reception in his honour at the church hall, a greying Miss Hawkesworthy ushered him to a quiet corner of the room to present him with a cardboard box. Her face carried the hallmarks of mischief as he pulled the flaps apart. His body froze when he revealed a ball of sea-washed hessian.

"Bill Llewellyn and myself, we think you're mature enough now to learn the truth, David," she said. He stared hard at her, eyes wide and mouth open.

"He didn't sell it, then?"

She shook her head. "No, he didn't, but he was so impressed with your faith that he rallied the shopkeepers together. They opened a fund and you know the result."

He bowed his head as the boyhood memories raced before him.

"I've never forgotten that episode of my life, it moulded my whole future, but why didn't he sell it?"

Her face broadened into a smile.

"Well, David, he wouldn't have got much for a lump of ship engine grease, would he?"

THE END

ISIS publish a wide range of books in large print, from fiction to biography. Any suggestions for books you would like to see in large print or audio are always welcome. Please send to the Editorial Department at:

ISIS Publishing Ltd.
7 Centremead
Osney Mead
Oxford OX2 0ES
(01865) 250 333

A full list of titles is available free of charge from:
Ulverscroft Large Print Books

(UK)
The Green
Bradgate Road, Anstey
Leicester LE7 7FU
Tel: (0116) 236 4325

(Australia)
P.O Box 953
Crows Nest
NSW 1585
Tel: (02) 9436 2622

(USA)
1881 Ridge Road
P.O Box 1230, West Seneca,
N.Y. 14224-1230
Tel: (716) 674 4270

(Canada)
P.O Box 80038
Burlington
Ontario L7L 6B1
Tel: (905) 637 8734

(New Zealand)
P.O Box 456
Feilding
Tel: (06) 323 6828

Details of **ISIS** complete and unabridged audio books are also available from these offices. Alternatively, contact your local library for details of their collection of **ISIS** large print and unabridged audio books.

Glorious Poverty
Derek Brock

In his inimitable way, Derek Brock recounts his early life, from his first memory onwards.

Born in 1933, in Culverhouse Cross near Cardiff, he was raised in Barry where his family struggled for food, clothes and heating. Nevertheless, there were moments of high comedy, tragedy, drama and serious learning.

At ten, Derek decides to contribute to the family finances, and begun his long career of job-seeking. Starting as an errand boy, he progressed through marine engineering, the railways, salesman, budding politician, eventually rising to become on of the script-writers for the *Goon Show*. However, he abandoned London to take over the pub made famous in *Cuckoo Marans in the Tap Room*.

A Double Thread
A Childhood in Mile End - and beyond
John Gross

John Gross is the son of a Jewish doctor who practised in the East End from the 1920s through the Second World War and beyond. His parents were steeped in the customs and traditions of Eastern Europe, yet outside the home, he grew up in a very English world of comics and corner shops, sandbags and bombsites, battered school desks and addictive, dusty cinemas.

Looking back on his childhood, he traces this double inheritance. The customs that underpinned family life — Yiddish stories and jokes, the rituals and mysteries of the synagogue — is set against the life of the streets, where gangsters are heroes and patients turn up on the door-step at all hours.